The Man Who Folded Himself

The Man Who Folded Himself

David Gerrold

Random House: New York

This book is for Larry Niven, a good friend who believes that time travel is impossible. He's probably right.

The Man Who Folded Himself

Oh wad some power the giftie gie us
To see oursels as others see us!
It wad frae monie a blunder free us,
  An' foolish notion.

—*Robert Burns*
To a Louse, stanza 8

* * *

In the box was a belt. And the following manuscript.

* * *

I hadn't seen Uncle Jim in months.

He looked terrible. His skin hung in wrinkled folds, his complexion was gray, and he was thin and stooped. He seemed to have aged ten years. Twenty. The last time I'd seen him, we were almost the same height. Now I realized I was taller.

"Uncle Jim!" I said. "Are you all right?"

He shook off my arm. "I'm fine, Danny. Just a little tired, that's all." He came into my apartment. His gait was no longer a stride, but more of a shuffle. He lowered himself to the couch with a sigh.

"Can I get you anything?"

He shook his head. "No, I don't have that much time. We have some important business to take care of— How old are you, boy?" He peered at me carefully.

"Huh—? I'm nineteen. You know that."

"Ah." He seemed to find that satisfactory. "Good. I was afraid I was too early, you looked so young—" He stopped himself. "How are you doing in school?"

"Fine." I said it noncommittally; the university was a bore. But Uncle Jim was paying me to attend. Three hundred dollars a week, plus my apartment and my car. And an extra hundred a week for keeping my nose clean.

"You don't like it though, do you?"

I said, "No, I don't." Why try to tell him I did? He'd know it for the lie it was.

"You want to drop out?"

I shrugged. "I could live without it."

"Yes," he agreed. "You could. Do you know how much you're worth right now?"

"No. How much?"

He pursed his lips thoughtfully; the wrinkled skin folded and unfolded. "One hundred and forty-three million dollars."

I whistled. "You're kidding."

"I'm not kidding."

"That's a lot of money."

"It's been properly handled."

One hundred and forty-three million dollars—! "Where is it now?" I asked. Stupid question.

"In stocks, bonds, properties. Things like that."

"I can't touch it then, can I?"

He looked at me and smiled. "I keep forgetting, Dan, how impatient you were—are." He corrected himself, then looked at me; his gaze wavered slightly. "You don't need it right now, do you?"

I thought about it. One hundred and forty-three million dollars. Even if they delivered it in fifties, the apartment wasn't that big. "No, I guess not."

"Then we'll leave it where it is." He added, "But it's your money. If you need it, you can have it."

4

One hundred and forty-three million dollars. What would I do with it—what *couldn't* I do with it? I had known my parents had left me a little money, but—

One hundred and forty-three million—!

I found I was having trouble swallowing.

"I thought it was in trust until I was twenty-five," I said.

"No," he corrected. "It's for me to administer for you until you're ready for it. You can have it any time you want."

"I'm not so sure I want it," I said slowly. "No—I mean, of course, I want it! It's just that—" How to explain? I had visions of myself trapped in a big mansion surrounded by butlers and bodyguards whose sole duty was to make sure that I dusted the stacks of bills every morning. One hundred and forty-three million dollars. Even in hundreds, it would fill several closets. "I'm doing okay on four hundred a week," I said. "All that more—"

"Four hundred a week?" Uncle Jim frowned; then, "Yes, I keep forgetting— There's been so much— Dan, I'm going to increase your allowance to a thousand dollars a week, but I want you to do something to earn it."

"Sure," I said, delighted in spite of myself. This was a sum of money I could understand. (One hundred and forty-three million—I wasn't sure there was that much money in the world; but a thousand dollars, yes, I could count to a thousand.) "What do I have to do?"

"Keep a diary."

"A diary?"

"That's right."

"You mean write things down in a black book every day? Dear diary, today I kissed a girl and all that kind of stuff?"

"Not exactly. I want you to record the things that seem important to you. Type out a few pages every day, that's all. You can record specific incidents or just make general comments about anything worth recording. All I want is your guarantee that you'll add something to it every day —or let's say at least once a week."

"And you want to read it—?" I started to ask.

"Oh, no, no, no—" he said hastily. "I just want to know that you're keeping it up. You won't have to show it to me. It's your diary. What you do with it or make of it is up to you."

My mind was working—a thousand dollars a week. "Can I use a dictation machine and a secretary?"

He shook his head. "It has to be a *personal* diary, Dan; that's the whole purpose of it. If it has to pass through someone else's hands, you might be inhibited. I want you to be honest." He straightened up where he sat, and for a moment he looked like the Uncle Jim I remembered, tall and strong. "Don't play any games, Dan—be truthful in your diary; if you're not, you'll only be cheating yourself. And put down everything—everything that seems important to you."

"Everything," I repeated dumbly.

He nodded. There was a lot of meaning in that word.

"All right," I said. "But why?"

"'Why?'" He looked at me. "You'll find out when you write it."

As usual, he was right.

* * *

There's a point beyond which money is redundant.

This is not something I discovered just this week. I've suspected it for a long time.

Four hundred dollars a week "spending money" gives a person a considerable amount of freedom to do whatever he wants. Within limits, of course—but those limits are wide enough to be not very restricting. Increase them to a thousand dollars a week and you don't feel them at all. The difference is hardly noticeable. Really.

Okay, so I bought some new clothes and records and a couple other fancy toys I'd had my eye on—but I'd already gotten used to having as much money as I'd needed (or wanted), so having that much more in my pocket really didn't make all that difference.

I had to start wearing bigger pockets, that's all.

Well—

I like to travel too. Usually, about once or twice a month I'd fly up to San Francisco for the weekend, or something like that. Palm Springs, Santa Barbara, Newport, San Diego. Follow the sun, that's me.

Since Uncle Jim increased my allowance, I've been to Acapulco, New York, and the Grand Bahamas. And I'm thinking about Europe. But it's not all that fun to travel alone—and nobody I know can afford to come along with me.

So I find I'm staying home just as much as before.

I could buy things if I wanted—but I've never cared much about owning things. They need to be dusted. Besides, I have what I need.

Hell, I have what I *want*—and that's more than what I need. I have everything I want now.

Big deal.

I think it's a bore.

*   *   *

I didn't exactly drop out of the university—I just sort of faded away.

It was a bore too.

I found I had less and less to say to my classmates. I call them my classmates because I'm not sure they were ever my friends. We weren't talking on the same levels.

Typical conversation: "—can I borrow five bucks, is she a good lay, does anyone know where I can score a lid, can you spare a quarter, I couldn't get my car running, do you know anyone who's had her, my ten o'clock class is a bitch, lend me a buck willya, what're we gonna do this weekend—"

They couldn't sympathize with my problems either.

"Problems? With a thousand dollars a week, who's got problems?"

Me.

I think.

I know something is wrong—I'm not happy. I wish I knew why.

I wonder if Uncle Jim is trying to teach me something.

*   *   *

I think I will tell this just exactly as it happened and try to do it without crying. If I can.

Uncle Jim is dead.

I got the phone call at eleven this morning. It was one of the lawyers from his company, Biggs or Briggs or something like that. He said, "Daniel Eakins?"

I said, "Yes?"

He said, "This is Jonathan Biggs-or-Briggs-or-something-like-that and I have some bad news for you about your uncle."

"My—uncle—" I must have wavered. Everything seemed made of ice.

The man was trying to be gentle. And not doing a very good job of it. He said, "He was found this morning by his maid—"

"He's—dead?"

"I'm sorry. Yes."

Dead? Uncle Jim?

"How—? I mean—"

"He just didn't wake up. He was a very old man—"

Old?

No—! It couldn't be. I wouldn't accept it. Uncle Jim was immortal.

"We thought that you—as next of kin—would like to supervise the funeral arrangements—"

Funeral arrangements?

"—on the other hand, we realize your distress at a time like this, so we've taken the liberty of—"

Dead? Uncle Jim?

The telephone was still making noises. I hung it up.

* * *

The funeral was a horror. Some idiot had decided on an open-casket ceremony, "so the deceased's family and friends might view him one more time."

Family and friends. Meaning me. And the lawyers. No one else.

I was surprised at that. And a little disappointed. I'd thought Uncle Jim was well known and popular. But there was nobody there—apparently I was the only one who cared.

Uncle Jim looked like hell. They had rouged his cheeks in a sickly effort to make him look like he was only asleep. It didn't work; it didn't disguise the fact that he was a shriveled and tired old hulk. I must have stared in horror. If he had seemed shrunken the last time I had seen him, today he looked positively emaciated. Used up.

No. Uncle Jim wasn't in that casket. That was just a piece of dead meat. Whatever it was that had made it Uncle Jim, that was gone—this empty old husk was nothing.

I bawled like a baby anyway.

The lawyers drove me home. I was moving like a zombie.

Everything seemed so damnably the same—it had all happened too fast, I hadn't had time to realize what it might mean, and now here was some dark-suited stranger sitting in my living room and trying to tell me that things were going to be different.

Different—? Without Uncle Jim, how could they be the same?

Biggs-or-Briggs-or-something-like-that shuffled some papers and managed to look both embarrassed and sorrowful.

I said, "I think I have some idea. I spoke with Uncle Jim a few weeks ago."

"Ah, good," he said. "Then we can settle this a lot easier." He hesitated. "Dan—Daniel, your uncle died indigent." I must have looked puzzled. He added, "That means *poor.*"

"What?" I blurted. "Now, wait a minute—that's not what he told me—"

"Eh? What did he tell you?"

I thought back. No, the lawyer was right. Uncle Jim hadn't said a word about his own money. Carefully I explained, "Uncle Jim said that *I* had a bit of money . . . and he was supposed to administer it. So naturally, I assumed that he had some of his own—or that he was taking a fee—"

Biggs-or-Briggs shook his head. "Your uncle *was* taking a fee," he said, "but it was only a token. You haven't got that much yourself."

"How much?" I asked.

"A little less than six thousand."

"Huh?"

"Actually, it's about five thousand nine hundred and something. I don't remember the exact amount." He shuffled papers in his briefcase.

I stared at him. "What happened to the hundred and forty-three million?"

He blinked. "I beg your pardon—?"

I felt like a fool, but repeated, "A hundred and forty-three million dollars. Uncle Jim said I had a hundred and forty-three million dollars. What happened to *that?*"

"A hundred and forty-three mill—" He pushed his glasses back onto his nose. "Uh, Mr. Eakins, you have six thousand dollars. That's all. I don't know where you got the idea that you had anything like—"

I explained patiently, "My Uncle Jim sat there, right where you're sitting now, and told me that I was worth one hundred and forty-three million dollars and that I could have it any time I wanted." I fixed him with what I hoped was my fiercest look. "Now, where is it?"

It didn't faze him at all. Instead he put on his I'd-better-humor-him expression. "Now, Daniel—Dan, I think you can understand that when a person gets old, his mind starts to get a little—well, funny. Your Uncle Jim may have told you that you were rich—he may even have believed it himself, but—"

"My Uncle Jim was not senile," I said. My voice was cold. "He may have been sick, but when I saw him, his mind was as clear as—as mine."

Biggs-or-Briggs looked like he wanted to reply to that, but didn't. Probably he was reminding himself that we'd just come from a funeral and I couldn't be expected to be entirely rational. "Well," he said. "The fact remains that all you have is six thousand dollars. To tell the truth, we were a little concerned with the way you've been spending these past few weeks—but your explanation clears that up. There's been a terrible misunderstanding—"

"Yes, there has. I want to see your books. When my parents died, their money was put in trust for me. It couldn't be all gone by now."

"Mr. Eakins—" he said. I could see that he was forcing himself to be gentle. "I don't know anything about your parents. It was your Uncle Jim who set up your trust fund, nineteen and a half years ago. He hasn't added to it since; that hasn't been necessary. His intention was to provide you with enough money to see you to your twenty-first birthday." He cleared his throat apologetically. "We almost made it. If he hadn't instructed us to increase your allowance two months ago, we probably could have made it stretch—"

I was feeling a little ill. This lawyer was making *too much* sense. When I thought of the spending I'd been doing—ouch! I didn't want to think about it.

Of course, I hadn't spent it all—I hadn't been trying. I started going over in my mind how much I thought I had left. Not that much, after all. Maybe a few hundred.

And six thousand left in trust. No hundred and forty-three million—

But Uncle Jim had said—

I stopped and thought about it. If I had really been worth a hundred and forty-three million dollars, would I have grown up the way I did? Brought up by a trained governess in Uncle Jim's comfortable—but not very big— San Fernando Valley home; sent to public schools and the State University? Uh-uh. Not likely.

If I'd been worth that big a pile, I'd have been fawned

over, drooled over, and protected every day of my life. I
would have had nurses and private tutors and valets and
chauffeurs. I would have had butlers for my butlers. I
would have had my own pony, my own yacht, my own
set of full-size trains. I would have had my pick of any
college in the country. In the world. I would have been
spoiled rotten.

I looked around my two-hundred-and-fifty-dollar-a-
month apartment. There was no evidence here that I was
spoiled rotten.

Well . . . not to the tune of a hundred and forty-three
million dollars.

You can get spoiled on four hundred a week, but that's
a far cry from butlers for your butlers.

Ouch. And ouch again.

I'd thought I'd never have to worry about money in
my life. Now I was wondering if I would make it to the
end of the year.

"—of course," Biggs-or-Briggs was mumbling, "if you
still feel you want to check our books, by all means—we
don't want there to be any misunderstandings or hard
feelings—"

"Yeah . . ." I waved it off. "I'll call you. There's no
hurry. I believe you, I guess." Maybe Uncle Jim *hadn't*
been thinking straight that day. The more I thought about
it, the odder his behavior seemed.

Oh, Uncle Jim! How could you have become so addled?
A hundred and forty-three million!

I wasn't sure whom I felt sorriest for, him or me.

The lawyer was still talking. "—Now, of course, you're
not responsible for any of his financial liabilities, and they
aren't that much anyway. The company will probably
cover them—"

"Wasn't there any insurance?" I blurted suddenly.

"Eh? No, I'm sorry. Your uncle didn't believe in it. We

tried to talk to him about that many times, but he never paid any attention."

I shrugged and let him go on. That was my Uncle Jim all over. Even *he* believed he was immortal.

"You're entitled to his personal effects and—"

"No, I don't want them."

"—there is one item he specifically requested you to have."

"What?"

"It's a package. Nobody's to open it but you."

"Well, where is it?"

"It's in the trunk of my car. If you'll just sign this receipt—"

* * *

I waited till after what's-his-name had left. Whatever it was in the box, Uncle Jim had intended it for me alone. I hefted it carefully. Perhaps *this* was the hundred and forty-three million—

I wondered—could you put that much money into a box this small?

Maybe it was in million-dollar bills, one hundred and forty-three of them. (I don't know—do they even print million-dollar bills?)

No, that couldn't be—could you imagine trying to cash one? I shuddered. Uh-uh, Uncle Jim wouldn't do that to me . . . well, let's see, maybe it was in ten-thousand-dollar bills. (That would be fourteen thousand, three hundred of them.) No, the box was too light—

If it *was* my fortune, it would have to be in some other form than banknotes. Rare postage stamps? Precious gems? Maybe— But I couldn't imagine a hundred and forty-three million dollars' worth of them, at least not in this box. It was too small.

There was only one way to find out. I ripped away the heavy brown wrapping paper and fumbled off the top.

It was a belt.

A black leather belt. With a stainless-steel plate for a buckle.

A belt.

I almost didn't feel like taking it out of the box. I felt like a kid at Santa Claus's funeral.

This was Uncle Jim's legacy?

I took it out. It wasn't a bad-looking belt—in fact, it was quite handsome. I wondered what I could wear it with—almost anything actually; it was that kind of style. It had a peculiar feel to it though; the leather flexed like an eel, as if it were alive and had an electric backbone running through it. The buckle too; it seemed heavier than it looked, and—well, have you ever tried to move the axis of a gyroscope? The torque resists your pressure. This belt buckle felt like that.

I looped it around my waist to see what it would look like. Not bad, but I had belts I liked better. I started to put it back in the box when it popped open in my hand. The buckle did.

I looked at the buckle more closely. What had looked like a single plate of stainless steel was actually two pieces hinged together at the bottom, so that when you were wearing the belt you could open it up and read the dials on the inside of the front.

Dials?

The thing had an electro-luminescent panel covered with numbers. It looked like a clock—it *was* a clock. The trademark on it said TIMEBELT. As I watched, two of the rows of numbers kept flickering, changing to keep track of the tenths of seconds, the seconds, and the minutes. Also indicated were the hours, the day, the month, the year—

Not bad if it was accurate, but I already had a watch and that was good enough. Besides, this seemed such a silly idea, putting a clock in a belt buckle. You'd feel embarrassed every time you opened it. Now, if it were a wristwatch—but whoever had built it probably couldn't have put that much circuitry into so small a space.

Fine. I had the world's only belt buckle that told the time. I started to close it up again—

Wait a minute—not so fast. I took a second look. There were *too many* numbers on that dial.

There were four rows of numbers, and a row of lights and some lettering. The whole thing looked like this:

[clr]			TIMEBELT				[act]
	AD	1975	May	21	13:06.43.09	
J	00	0000	000	00	00 00 00 00	F
0000000000000000000000000000000000000							
T	AD	1975	May	21	13:06.43.09	B
	AD	1975	Mar	16	17:30.00.00	
[hol]			TIMEBELT				[ret]

Odd. What were all those numbers for?

The date on the bottom, for instance: March 16, 1975—what was so special about that? What had happened at 5:30 on March 16?

I frowned; there *was* something—

I went looking for my calendar. Yes, there it was. March 16: *Uncle Jim coming at 5:30.*

The date on the bottom was the last time I had seen Uncle Jim! March 16! He had knocked on the door precisely at 5:30!

Uncle Jim was always punctual when he made appointments. On the phone he had said he would be at my place at 5:30—sure enough, he was. But why, six months later, was that date so important as to be on his calendar belt? It didn't make sense.

And there was something else I hadn't noticed. The other part of the buckle—the side facing the clock—was divided into buttons. There were four rows of them, all square and flush with each other. The top row was cut into two; the second row, six; the third row, three; and the bottom row, six again.

My curiosity was piqued. Now, what were *these* for?

I touched one of the top two. The letter B on the lower right side of the panel began to glow. I touched it again and the letter F above it winked on instead. All right—but what did they mean?

I put the belt around my waist and fastened it. Actually, it fastened itself; the back of the clasp leaped against the leather part and held. I mean, *held*. I tugged at it, but it didn't slip. Yet I could pop it off as easily as separating two magnets. Quite a gimmick that.

The buckle was still open; I could read the numbers on it easily. Almost automatically my hand moved to the buttons. Yes, that was right—the buttons were a keyboard against my waist, the panel was the readout; the whole thing was a little computer.

But what in hell was I computing?

Idly I touched some of the buttons. The panel blinked. One of the dates changed. I pressed another button and the center row of lights flickered. When I pressed the first button again, a different part of the date changed. I didn't understand it, and there was nothing in the box except some tissue paper.

Maybe there was something on the belt itself. I took it off.

On the back of the clasp, it said:

TIMEBELT
TEMPORAL TRANSPORT
DEVICE

Temporal Transport Device—? Hah! They had to be kidding.

A time machine? In a belt? Ridiculous.

And then I found the instructions.

＊　＊　＊

The instructions were on the back of the clasp—when I touched it lightly, the words TIMEBELT, TEMPORAL TRANSPORT DEVICE winked out and the first "page" of directions appeared in their place. Every time I tapped it after that, a new page appeared. They were written in a kind of linguistic shorthand, but they were complete. The table of contents ran on for several pages itself:

OPERATION OF THE TIMEBELT
  Understanding
  Theory and Relations
  Time Tracking
  The Paradox Paradox
  Alternity
  Discoursing

ARTIFACTING
  Transporting
  Special Cases
  Cautions

I was beginning to feel a little dazed—of course this couldn't be for real. It couldn't be . . .

I sat down on the couch and began reading the directions in detail. They were easy to understand. There was a great deal about the principles of operation and the variety of uses, but I just skimmed that. First I wanted to find out *how* the belt worked, perhaps even try it . . .

The readout panel was easy enough to understand. The top row of numbers was the time *now;* the second row was the distance you wished to travel away from it, either forward or back; and the third row was the moment to which you were traveling, your target. The fourth row was the date of your last jump—that is, *when* the belt had last come from. (Later I found that it could also be the date of the next jump if you had preprogrammed for it. Or it could be a date held in storage—one that you could keep permanently set up and jump to at a moment's decision.)

The letters F and B on the right side, of course, stood for *Forward* and *Back*. The letters J and T on the left side stood for *Jump* and *Target*. The lights in the center of the panel had several functions; mostly they indicated the belt's programming.

In each corner of the readout was a lettered square. These were references to four buttons on the face of the buckle itself. (I closed the buckle and looked—there weren't any *obvious* buttons, but in each corner was an area that seemed to depress with a slight click.) CLR stood for *Clear*, HOL meant *Hold*, RET was *Return*, and ACT was *Activate*. Each button had to be pressed twice in rapid succession to function; that way you wouldn't accidentally change any of your settings or send yourself off on an unintended jaunt.

CLR was meant to clear the belt of all previous instructions and settings. HOL would hold any date in storage indefinitely, or call it out again. RET would send you back to the moment of your last jump, or to any date locked in by HOL. ACT would do just that—*act*. Whatever instructions had been programmed into the belt, nothing would happen until ACT was pressed. Twice.

There were more instructions. There was something called Timestop and something else called Timeskim. According to the instructions, each was an interrupted time jump resulting in a controlled out-of-phase relationship with the real-time universe. Because the rate of phase congruency could be controlled, so could the perceived rate of the timestream.

What that meant was that I could view events like a motion picture film. I could speed it up and see things happening at an ultra-fast rate via the Timeskim, or I could freeze them altogether with the Timestop.

The Timeskim was necessary to allow you to maintain your bearings over a long-range jump; you could skim *through* time instead of jumping directly. The movement of people and animals would be a blur, but you would be able to avoid materializing inside of a building that hadn't been there before. The Timestop was intended to help you get your bearings after you arrived, but before you reinserted yourself into the timestream, especially if you were looking for a particular moment. With everything seemingly frozen solid, you could find an unobserved place to appear, or you could remain an unseen observer of the Timestopped still life. Or you could Timeskim at the real-time rate without being a part of real-world events, again an unseen observer. I guessed that

the Timestop and Timeskim were necessary for traveling to unfamiliar eras—especially dangerous ones.

There were other functions too, complex things that I
didn't understand yet. I decided to leave them alone for
a while. For instance, Entropy Awareness left me a bit
leery. I concentrated on the keyboard instead. After all,
programming the belt was the most important part.

The top two buttons controlled Jump and Target, Forward and Back. The second row of six controlled any six
digits of the date; the third row of three was for programming—they determined the settings of the second and
fourth rows. The fourth row had six buttons; used in com-
bination with the third row, they determined eighteen
different functions. When the top two buttons were used
too, there were seventy-two different ways of using the
belt. Maybe more. Each of the buttons on the keyboard
was multi-functional. What it controlled and how was
determined by which other buttons it was used in com-
bination with.

Clearly this timebelt was not a simple device. There
was a lot to learn.

* * *

I felt like a kid with a ten-dollar bill in a candy store—no,
like an adolescent with a hundred-dollar bill in a brothel.

I was ready—but what should I do first?

Possibilities cascaded across my mind like a stack of un-
opened presents. I was both eager and scared. My hand
was nervous as I fumbled open the buckle.

I eyed the readout plate warily. All the numbers had
been cleared and were at zero; they gazed right back at
me.

Well, let's try something simple first. I touched the third button in the third row, setting the second row of controls for minutes, seconds and tenths of seconds. I tapped the first button in the second row twice: twenty minutes. I set the top right-hand button for Forward, the top left-hand button for Jump.

I double-checked the numbers on the panel and closed the belt.

Now. All I had to do was tap the upper right-hand corner of the buckle twice.

The future waited.

I swallowed once and tapped.

—*POP!*—

I staggered and straightened. I had forgotten about that. The instructions had warned that there would be a slight shock every time I jumped. It had something to do with forcing the air out of the space you were materializing in. It wasn't bad though—I just hadn't been expecting it. It was like scuffing your shoes on a rug and then touching metal, that kind of shock, but all over your whole body at once.

Aside from that, I had no way of proving I was in the future.

Oh, wait. Yes, I did. I was still wearing my wristwatch. It said 1:43. I strode into the kitchen and looked at the kitchen clock.

It said 2:03.

That's when it hit me—I had *actually* traveled through time! Twenty minutes forward! I actually had!

Until now I'd been treating the whole thing as a game; not even the jump-shock had convinced me. That could have been faked by a battery in the belt. But this—! I *knew* my watch and I *knew* that kitchen clock; they couldn't have been faked.

I actually had a time machine. A real live, honest-to-God *working* time machine.

I took a deep breath and forced myself to be calm. I *tried* to force myself to be calm.

I had a time machine. A real time machine. I had jumped twenty minutes forward. The room looked just the same, not even the quality of the afternoon sunlight had changed, but I knew I had jumped forward in time. The big question was *what was I going to do next?*

I had to think about this—no problem, I had all the time in the world. I giggled when I realized that.

Hmm. I knew. Suddenly I realized what I could do.

I opened the belt and reset the control for twenty-four hours. Forward. I would pick up a copy of tomorrow's paper, then bounce back and go to the race track today. I would make a fortune. I would—

MIGOD! Why hadn't I realized this—?

I could be as rich as I wanted to be.

Rich—! The word lost all meaning when I realized what I could do. Not just the race track—Las Vegas! The stock market! Anything! There were boxing matches to bet on and companies to invest in, new products from the future and rare objects from the past—my head swam with the possibilities.

I wanted to laugh. And I'd been worried about a *mere* hundred and forty-three million dollars!

Uncle Jim had been right after all! I *was* rich! I wanted to shout! I felt like dancing! The room twirled with wealth and I spun with it—until I tripped over a chair.

Still gasping and giggling, I sat up. It was too much—too much!

Before—before I had proven that the belt really worked—all those possibilities had been merely fantasies: fun things to think about, but not taken seriously. Now, however, they were *more* than possibilities. They were *probabilities.* I would do them all. All! I had all the time in the world! I was hysterical with delight. Giddy with enthusiasm—

I forced myself to stop.

Be serious now, I told myself. Let's approach this properly. Let's think these things out; take them one at a time—

Tomorrow. I grinned and touched the button.

—*Pop!*—

* * *

This time the shock wasn't so bad, I—

—*There was somebody in the room.* I started. Then he turned to face me.

For a moment it was like staring into a sudden mirror—

He said, "I've been waiting for you."

It was me.

I must have been staring, because he said, "Relax, Dan—" and I jumped again.

The sound of his voice—it was *my* voice as I've heard it on tape. The look in his eyes—I've seen those eyes in my mirror. His face—it was my face—the features, everything: the nose, short and straight; the hair, dark brown with a hint of red and with the wave that I can't comb out; the mouth, wide and smiling; the cheekbones, high and pronounced.

"You're me—" It must have sounded inane.

He was a little flustered too. He held out something he had been holding, a newspaper. "Here," he said. "I believe we were going to the races."

"We?"

"Well, it's no fun going alone, is it?"

26

"Uh—" My head was still spinning.

"It's all right," he said. "I'm *you*—I'm your future self. Tomorrow you'll be me. That is, we're the same person; we've just doubled back our timeline."

"Oh," I said, blinking.

He grinned. "I'll be your twin brother."

I looked at him again; he stared unabashedly back. He was almost delighting in my confusion, and he had hit on one of my most secret fantasies. Of course! He couldn't help but know—he was me! When I had been younger, my greatest desire had been the impossible wish for an identical twin—a second me, someone whom I could talk to and share secrets with. Someone who would always be there so I would never be alone. Someone who—

I gaped helplessly. It was all happening too fast.

He reached out and took my hand, shook it warmly. "Hi," he said. "I'm Don. I'm your brother." At first I just let him shake my hand, but after a second of his smiling at me, I returned his grip. (Interesting—some people shake my hand and their grip is too hard. Others have a grip that's too weak. Don's grip was just right—but why shouldn't it be? *He's me.* I have to keep reminding myself of that; it's almost too easy to think of him as Don.) The touch of his hand was strange—is that what I feel like?

We went to the races.

Oh, first we bounced back twenty-eight hours; both of us. He flashed back first, then I followed. We both reappeared at the same instant because our target settings were identical. (He was wearing a timebelt too—well, of course; if I could be duplicated, so could the belt.) I couldn't shake the feeling that this fellow from the future was invading my home—even though it was meaningless—but he seemed so sure of himself that I had to follow in his wake.

When I glanced at the kitchen clock, I got another start. It was just a little past ten—why, I was still at Uncle Jim's funeral! I'd be coming home in an hour with the lawyer. Maybe it was a good thing that Don had taken the lead; there was still too much I didn't know.

As we walked out to the car, Mrs. Peterson, the old lady in the front apartment, was just coming out of her door. "Hello, Danny—" she started, then stopped. She looked from one to the other of us confusedly.

"This is my brother," said Don quickly. "Don," he said to me, a gentle pressure on my arm, "this is Mrs. Peterson." To her, "Don will be staying with me for a while, so if you think you're seeing double, don't be surprised."

She smiled at me. I nodded, feeling like a fool. *I* knew Mrs. Peterson—but Don's grip on my arm reminded me that *she didn't know*. She looked back and forth, blinking. "I didn't know you were twins—"

"We've been—living separately," said Don quickly, "so we could each have a chance to be our own person. Don's been up in San Francisco for the past two years."

"Oh," she said. She turned on her smile again and beamed politely at me. "Well, I hope you'll like it in Los Angeles, Don. There's so much to do."

"Uh—yes," I said. "It's very—exciting."

We made our goodbyes and went on to the car. Abruptly, Don started giggling. "I wish you could have seen your face," he said. "Well, you will—tomorrow." Still laughing, he repeated my last words, "'Uh—yes. It's very—exciting.' You looked as if you'd swallowed a frog."

I stopped in the act of unlocking the passenger-side door. (It seemed natural for him to take the driver's side; besides, I was unsure of the way to the track.) "Why didn't you let *me* explain?" I asked. "She's *my* neighbor."

"She's *my* neighbor too," he replied, giggling again. "Besides, what would you have said? At least I've been through this once before." He opened his door and dropped into the driver's seat.

I got in slowly and looked at him. He was unlatching the convertible top, preparatory to putting it down. He didn't notice my gaze. I realized that I was feeling resentful of him—he was so damned sure of himself, even to the way he was making himself at home in my car. Was that the way I was? I found myself studying his mannerisms.

"Put on a tape," he said, indicating the box of cassettes on the floor. He started to name one, then stopped himself. "Want me to tell you what you're going to choose?"

"Uh—no, thanks." I studied the different titles with such an intensity I couldn't see any of them. It would be impossible for me to surprise him—no matter what tape I chose, no matter what I did, he would already *know,* he would have done it himself.

Of course, he had been through all this before. He had every reason to be sure of himself. When I became him, I'd probably be cocky too. Perhaps a little giddy—you couldn't help but feel powerful if you knew everything that was going to happen before it happened.

Of course he should be the one to do the talking.

Later I'd get my turn; but right now I was feeling a little unsure, both of myself and of the situation. I could learn by following his lead. I put on a tape of *Petrouchka* and concentrated on the road.

I'd never been to the race track before. It was bigger than I'd expected. Don steered his way into the parking lot with surprising familiarity and arrowed immediately toward a space that shouldn't have been there, but was.

Instead of seats in the bleachers, as I had expected, he bought a private box. Grinning at me, he explained, "Why not? We deserve the best."

I wanted to point out that it wasn't necessary; besides,

it cost too much. Then I realized he was right; the money made no difference at all. We were going to make a lot more than we spent, so why not enjoy? I shut up and let myself be awed by the great expanses of green lawn. Under the bright sun, the wide sweeping track seemed poised in midair, a curve of stark and simple elegance. The stands loomed high above us and I was properly impressed.

We ordered mint juleps from the bar—*nouveau riche* I thought, but didn't protest—and made our way to our seats. Don made a great show of studying the paper, which I thought was funny—it was *today's* race results he was poring over. "Yes, yes . . ." he muttered in loud tones of stentorian thoughtfulness. "I think Absolam's Ass looks pretty good in the first." He looked up. "Danny, go put a hundred dollars on Absolam's Ass. To win."

"Uh—" I started fumbling in my pockets. "I only have sixty—" And then I broke off and looked at him. "A hundred dollars—?" On a horse? A hundred dollars?

He was eying me with cool amusement. There was a crisp new bill in his hand. "You want to get rich?" he asked. "You have to risk money to make it."

I blinked and took the bill. Somehow I found my way to the betting windows and traded the money for ten bright printed tickets. The clerk didn't even glance up.

Absolam's Ass paid off at three to one. We now had three hundred dollars. Don ordered two more mint juleps while I went to collect our winnings and put them on Fig Leaf. This time the clerk hesitated, repeated the bet aloud, then punched the button on his machine.

Fig Leaf paid off at two to one. We now had six hundred dollars. And another mint julep.

Calamity Jane also paid off at two to one. We were up to twelve hundred dollars, and the clerk at the window was beginning to recognize me.

Finders Keepers came in second, and I looked at Don in consternation. He merely grinned and said, "Wait—" I waited, and Harass was disqualified for bumping Tumbleweed. Finders Keepers paid eight to one. Ninety-six hundred dollars. The betting official went a little goggle-eyed when I tried to put it all on Big John. He had to call over the track manager to okay it.

Big John came in at three to one. Twenty-eight thousand, eight hundred dollars. *I* was getting a little goggle-eyed. The track manager personally took my next bet; with that much money at stake, I couldn't blame him. I made a little show of hesitating thoughtfully as if I couldn't make up my mind, partly to keep him from getting curious about my "system" and partly because I was getting nervous about all the people who were watching me to see which way I would bet. Apparently they were betting the same way. Word of my "luck" seemed to have spread. (I didn't like that—I'd heard somewhere that too much money on one horse could change the odds. Well, no matter. As long as I still won . . .)

As I climbed back to our seats, I thought I saw Don leaving, but I must have been mistaken because he was still sitting there in our box. When he saw me, he folded the newspaper he'd been looking at and shoved it under his seat. I started to ask him about the odds, but he said, "Don't worry about it. We're leaving right after this race. We're through for the day."

"Huh—? Why?"

He waited until the horses broke from the gate; the crowd roared around us. "Because in a few minutes we're going to be worth fifty-seven thousand, six hundred dollars. Don't you think that's enough?"

"But if we keep going," I protested, "we can win almost a million dollars on an eight-horse parlay."

He flinched at that. "There are better ways to make a

million dollars," he said. "Quieter ways, more discreet."

I didn't answer. Evidently he knew something I didn't. I watched as Michelangelo crossed the finish line and paid off at two to one. Don scooped up his two newspapers and stood. "Come on," he said. "You go get the money. I'll wait for you at the car."

I was a little disappointed that he didn't want to come with me to collect our winnings; after all, they were as much his as they were mine. (I'm getting my tenses confused—they were all *mine*, but it seemed like *ours*.) Didn't he care about the money?

No matter. I found my way down to the windows to turn my tickets in—that is, I *tried* to turn my tickets in. There were some forms to be filled out first, and a notification for the Bureau of Internal Revenue. And I had to show my driver's license for identification and my credit cards too. The track manager was beaming at me and kept shaking my hand and wanting to know if I would please stay around for the photographers and reporters.

At first I was pleased with the idea, but something inside me went *twang*—just a warning sensation, that's all, but it was enough. "I don't want any publicity," I said; now I knew why Don had beaten such a hasty retreat.

I shook off the track manager and collected my check for $57,600 as quickly as possible. It felt like a mighty powerful piece of paper; I was almost afraid to put it in my pocket. I must have walked out to the parking lot like my pants were on fire. I was that nervous and excited.

Don was sitting on the passenger side, looking thoughtful. I was too giddy to notice. "You want to see the check?" I asked, waving it at him.

He shook his head, "I've already seen it." Then he pulled it out of his pocket to show me—*his* check for $57,600! He'd had it with him all the time!

I blinked from one to the other. They were identical, even down to the last curlicue on the signature.

"Hey!" I said. "Two checks! Why don't we cash them both?"

Don looked at me. "We can't. Think about it. If you cash yours, how do I get it back so I can cash it?"

He was right, of course. I wanted to hit myself for being so stupid. It was the same check. He—I—we just hadn't cashed it yet. He slipped it back into his pocket; I did the same with mine. Well, at least it was nice to know I wasn't going to lose it.

*　　*　　*

I drove home. Don was strangely quiet; I noticed it almost immediately because I had gotten used to letting him do all the talking. (After all, there was no point in my saying anything; he already knew it, and anything I needed to know, he would tell me.) But now he had lost his former exuberance. He seemed almost—brooding.

I was still too excited by the whole experience. I couldn't *stop* talking. But after a bit I began to realize it was a one-sided conversation. I trailed off, feeling foolish. (He'd heard it all before, I had to remind myself. After all, he'd said it too.)

"Well," I said. "What happens now? Do you go back to your time?"

He looked at me, forced himself to smile. "Not yet. First we go out to celebrate. Like rich people."

Of course. It's not every day you make $57,600.

We stopped at home to change clothes. (There was a bit of hassling over who was going to use the bathroom first and who was going to wear whose favorite sport jacket, but eventually we compromised. Even so, this was something I might have trouble getting used to—sharing my life. I like to live alone, and this business of another person—even when *it's only yourself*—sharing your apartment, your clothes, your bathroom, your razor, your toothbrush, and *even* your clean underwear, can be unnerving. To say the least.)

The restaurant was called simply *The* Restaurant. It's supposed to be one of the best places in the city, but I'd never been there before, so I didn't know. Don, of course, was quite familiar with the layout. He presented himself to the maître d' and announced, "You have a reservation for Mr. Daniel Eakins . . . ?"

Yes, he did—When had Don arranged that?—and led us to a table on a balcony overlooking a splashing fountain. Fancy.

We started off with cocktails, of course, and an hors d'oeuvre tray that was a meal in itself, and then had another drink while we studied the menu and wine list. I went goggle-eyed at the prices, mostly out of habit, but Don merely announced, "Last night I had the steak. Today I'm going to try the lobster."

His "last night" was my tonight. I had steak.

It was still early in the evening. We were in a quiet and empty corner. Somewhere a violinist was teasing with a Bach concerto. I sipped my drink and studied Don; I was beginning to find his self-assurance attractive. (I knew what that meant. I wanted to be the same way, and I'd begin to imitate him.)

He was studying me too, but there was a detached smile on his lips. I could tell his thoughts were not running the same course as mine and I wondered what he was thinking about. I kept looking at him and he kept looking back at me.

Finally I had to break away. "I can't get used to this,"

I said. "I mean, I thought I'd be doing all this alone. I didn't realize that you'd be here—"

"But why should you have to be alone?" He'd started to answer my question before I'd finished asking it. "You'll never have to be alone again. You'll always have me. I'll always have you. It makes more sense this way—I don't like being alone either. This way I can share the things I like with somebody I know likes them too. I don't have to try and impress you, you don't have to try and impress me; there's perfect understanding, there'll never be any of those destructive little head games that people play on each other, because we're a perfect match. I like *me*, Danny, that's why I like *you*. You'll feel the same way, you'll see. And I guarantee, there are no two people in this world who understand each other as well as we do."

"Um—" I said. I studied the pattern of bread crumbs on the tablecloth. Don's intensity scared me. All my life I had been a loner; I wasn't very good at talking to people, and when they tried to get too close to me, I backed away in a hurry.

(Uncle Jim had arranged for me to visit an analyst once. It hadn't worked. I wouldn't even open up for him. The most I would admit was a feeling that I wasn't living life, but operating it by remote control.) So now, when Don opened his thoughts to me—

—but I couldn't reject him. He was *me*. How could I put up a psychological barrier between myself? I couldn't, of course, but it was the candidness of Don's admissions which made me uncomfortable.

Abruptly, he was changing the subject. "Besides, there's another advantage," he pointed out. "With me along, you'll never be taken by surprise. Whatever we do, I'll have been through it before, so I'll know what to expect, and you'll be learning it at the hands of an expert guide. *Whatever* we do."

"I've always wanted to try parachute jumping," I offered.

He grinned, "Me too." Suddenly he was serious again. "When you go, Dan, you *have* to take me. I'm your insurance so you can't be killed."

"Huh?" I stared at him.

He repeated it. *"When you're with me, you can't be killed.* It's like the check this afternoon. If anything happens to the earlier one, the later one won't be there beside it—*it won't exist!* It's more than me just being able to warn you about things—my sitting here across from you is *proof* that you won't be killed before tomorrow night. And I know that nothing happens to *me"*—he thumped his chest to indicate which "me" he was talking about—"because I've got my memories. *I've* seen that nothing will happen to me tonight, so you're my insurance too."

I thought about that.

He was right.

"Remember the automobile accident we *didn't* have last year?"

I shuddered. I'd had a blowout on the San Diego Freeway while traveling at seventy miles an hour. It had been the left front tire and I had skidded across three lanes and found myself facing the wrong way, with traffic rushing at me. And the motor had stalled. I just barely had time to restart the engine and pull off to the side. It had been fifteen minutes before my hands stopped trembling enough for me to attempt changing the tire. It was a mess; for weeks afterward I'd kept a piece of it on the dashboard to remind me how close a call I'd had. I still had nightmares about it: if traffic had been just a little bit heavier . . . the sickening swerve-skid-bumpety-bump-screeeeeeech—

I figured I was living on borrowed time. I really should have been killed. Really. It was only a miracle that I hadn't been.

I realized my hand was shaking. I forced myself to take a sip of my drink. I looked at Don; he was as grim as I was. "There's too much to lose, isn't there?" he said.

I nodded. We shared the same memory. There was a lot we didn't have to say.

"Dan," he said; his tone was intense, as intense as before. His eyes fixed me with a penetrating look. "We're going to be more than just identical twins. We can't help it. We're closer than brothers."

I met his gaze, but the thought still frightened me.

I'm not sure I know how to be that close to anybody. Even myself.

*   *   *

We ate the rest of our dinner in silence, but it wasn't an uncomfortable silence; no, it was a peaceful one, relaxed.

I had to get used to the situation, and Don was letting me. He sat there and smiled a lot, and I got the feeling that he was simply enjoying my presence. I had to learn how to relax, that was the problem; other people had always unnerved me because I thought they were continually *judging* me. How do I look? What kind of a person do I seem? Is my voice firm enough? How am I standing? What does my posture say? Am I really intelligent or just pedantic? Was that joke really funny, or am I making a fool of myself? I worried about the impression I was making. If I was shy, did they think I was being aloof and call me a snob? If I tried to be friendly, did they find me overbearing? I feared that I was basically unlikable, so I wouldn't give them the chance to find out; or I tried too hard to be likable, and proved that I wasn't.

And yet—

Here was this person, Don, sitting across from me . . . he wasn't unlikable at all. In fact, he was quite attractive. Handsome, even. His face was ruddy and tanned (well, that was the sun lamp in the bathroom, but it looked good); his eyes were clear, almost glowing (that must be from the tinted contact lenses); his hair was carefully styled (that was the hair blower, of course)—he was everything I was always trying to be. His voice was firm, his manner was gentle, and he was in good physical condition. Perhaps I had been too hard in judging myself.

Yes, I liked the look of this person. He was capable, assured, and confident. He projected—likability. Friendliness.

And something else. There was that same kind of longing—no, maybe desperation is the word—in Don: that feeling of *reach out, touch me, here I am, please* that I so often felt in myself. Under his assurance was a hint of—helplessness?—need? And I could respond to that. I enjoyed his presence, but *more* than that, I sensed a feeling that he needed me. Yes, he needed to know that *I* liked *him*.

I realized I was smiling. It was nice to be needed, I decided. I was glowing, but not with the liquor. Not entirely. I was learning to love—no, I was learning to *like* myself. I was learning to relax with another person.

We spent a lot of time drinking and thinking and just looking at each other. And giggling conspiratorially. Our communication was empathic. We didn't need words—we simply enjoyed each other's existence.

After dinner we went to a nearby bar and played a few games of pool. It was one of the few things we could do that wouldn't be boring the second time around. Any kind of spectator entertainment, such as a movie or a show or a baseball game, would be too much to take two nights in a row, but participation activities would be just fine. Swimming, sailing, riding; I could learn from watching my own technique. (I wondered if I could get a poker game going—let's see, I'd need at least five of me. I doubted it would work, but it might be worth a try.)

We got home about eleven-thirty; we were holding each other up, we were that drunk. Don looked at me blearily. "Well, good night, Dan. I'll see you tomorrow— no, I'll see you the day after tomorrow. Tomorrow I have to see Don and *you* have to see Dan—" He frowned at that, went over it again in his head, looked at me again. "Yeah, that's right." He flipped open his belt buckle, set it, double-checked it, closed it, and vanished forward into time. The air gave a soft *pop!* as it rushed in to fill the space where he had been.

*   *   *

After he left I stumbled through the apartment, wondering what to do next—another trip through time? No. I decided not. I was too tired. First I'd get some sleep. If I could.

I paused to pick up the clothes that I'd scattered on the floor this afternoon when we'd changed for dinner; I realized I was picking up *his* clothes too—wait a minute, that meant that he'd left wearing some of *my* clothes.

I looked in the closet. Yes, the good sport jacket and

slacks that he'd borrowed were missing. So was my red tie. But the sweater and slacks that he'd discarded were still there.

No, they weren't—they were in my hand! I blinked back and forth between the clothes I was holding and the clothes in my closet. They were the same! I'd lost a jacket and slacks, but I'd gained a sweater and a pair of pants identical to ones I already owned. I had to figure this out.

Ah, I had it. The jacket and slacks he'd borrowed had traveled forward in time with him. They'd be waiting there for me when—no, that wasn't right. I'd be going back in time tomorrow—that is, I'd be coming back to today, where I'd pick them up and take them forward with me. Right. They'd just be skipping forward a few hours.

And the sweater and the other pair of pants—the duplicated ones—obviously, that's what I'd be wearing tomorrow when I bounced back, leaving only one set in the future. The condition of having two of them was only temporary, like the condition of having two of me. It was just an illusion.

Or was it?

What would happen if I wore *his* sweater and slacks back through time? The sweater and slacks that he brought from the future would then be the clothes that I would leave in the past so that I could put them on when I went back to the past to leave them there for myself, ad infinitum . . . and meanwhile, *my* sweater and slacks would be hanging untouched in the closet.

Or would they?

What would happen tomorrow if I *didn't* wear either sweater or pair of slacks? But something else entirely? (But how could I? I'd already seen that I *had* worn them.)

Would the pair that he brought back cease to exist? Or would they remain—would I have somehow duplicated them?

There was only one way to find out . . .

I fell asleep thinking about it.

* * *

The morning was hot, with that crisp kind of unreality that characterizes the northern edge of the San Fernando Valley. I awoke to the sound of the air conditioner already beginning its day's work with an insistent pressing hum.

For a while I just stared at the ceiling. I'd had the strangest dream—

—but it wasn't a dream. I bounced out of bed in sudden fear. The timebelt glittered on the dresser where I had left it. I held it tightly, as if it might fade abruptly away. All the excitement of yesterday flooded back into me.

I remembered. The race track. The restaurant. Don. The check. It was sitting on the dresser too, right next to the belt—$57,600.

I opened the belt and checked the time. It was almost eleven. I'd have to hurry. Don would be arriving—no, *I* was Don now. *Dan* would be arriving in three hours.

I showered and shaved, pulled on a sport shirt and slacks and headed for the car. I wanted to go to the bank and deposit the check and I had to pick up a newspaper—

Actually, I didn't need the newspaper at all, I could remember which horses had won without it, but there was a headline on the front page of the *Herald-Examiner*: FIVE-HORSE PARLAY WINS $57,600!

Huh—? I hadn't seen that before. But then, Don hadn't shown me the front page.

The story was a skimpy one and they'd misspelled my name; mostly it was about how much I had bet on each horse and how it had snowballed. Then there were some quotes from various track officials saying how pleased they were to have such a big winner (*I'll bet!*), especially because it helped publicize the sport (and probably attracted a lot of hopeful losers too.) Finally there was even a quote from me about what I was planning to do with the money: "I don't know yet, I'm still too excited. Probably I'll take a vacation. I've always wanted to see the world. I'd like to invest some of it too, but I have to wait and see what's left after taxes." Faked, of course. I hadn't spoken to any reporters at all; but apparently some editor had felt the story wouldn't be complete without a few words from the happy winner.

I was both pleased and annoyed. Pleased at being a "celebrity." Annoyed that they were putting words in my mouth. Maybe today we'd do it differently.

Could we?

Suppose we didn't stop at $57,600—suppose we went after an *eight*-horse parlay. That would be worth almost $750,000! Hmm. I thought about it all during breakfast at the local coffee shop.

Afterward I went to the bank—and found I'd forgotten the check at home. Damn! Well, I'd have to deposit it later. Instead I withdrew two hundred and fifty dollars from my savings account so we'd have some money for the track today.

I got home with time to spare. I decided to change into some cooler clothes—then I remembered the sweater and slacks. What *would* happen if I wore something else instead?

I went burrowing in the closet, found some lightweight trousers, a shirt and a windbreaker. They would do just fine. Now, what else was there I had to take care of?

Nothing that I could see. I scooped up the check and put it in my pocket; I didn't want to leave it lying around. Dan would be arriving at—

There was a soft *pop!* in the air.

I turned to see a startled-looking me.

"Hi," I said. "I've been waiting for you."

His eyes were wide; he looked positively scared. "Relax, Dan—" I said. He jumped when I spoke.

For a moment all he could do was stare, his face was a study in amazement. "You're me—"

I suddenly realized how silly this whole tableau was. I thrust the newspaper at him. "Here. I believe we were going to the races . . . ?"

"We?"

That's right—*he didn't know!* "Well, it's no fun going alone, is it?"

"Uh—"

"It's all right," I said. "I'm *you*—I'm your future self. Tomorrow you'll be me. That is, we're the same person; we've just doubled back our timeline."

He blinked. "Oh."

He looked so confused, I wanted to touch him. I smiled. "I'll be your twin brother." There was so much I wanted to explain. I wanted to tell him everything that Don had told me last night, but somehow it wasn't the right time. He was looking at me too hesitantly. Instead I reached out and took his hand, shook it firmly. "Hi," I said. "I'm Don. I'm your brother." After a bit he returned my grip. I think he was a little scared of me—but also curious.

We bounced back in time to his "today." (I snuck a peek in the closet when he wasn't looking. There was only one sweater and slacks—of course, I hadn't brought them back with me. But there was a duplicate of the trousers, shirt and windbreaker I was wearing now! So you *could* change the timestream . . . !)

On the way out to the car, old lady Peterson surprised us—surprised Danny, I should say; I'd been expecting her. "This is my brother," I said quickly. "Don"—I touched his arm—"this is Mrs. Peterson." To her, "Don will be staying with me for a while, so if you think you're seeing double, don't be surprised."

She smiled at us. "I didn't know you were twins—"

"We've been—living separately," I answered. "So we could each have a chance to be our own person. Don's been living up in San Francisco for the past two years."

"Oh," she said. She beamed politely at Dan. "Well, I hope you'll like it in Los Angeles, Don. There's so much to do."

He went kind of frog-faced at that; he managed to stammer out, "Uh—yes. It's very exciting."

I couldn't help myself. I started giggling; when we got to the car I couldn't hold it in any longer. "I wish you could have seen your face—" I said. Then I realized. "Well, you will—tomorrow." He was half glaring at me. "'Uh—yes. It's very exciting,'" I mocked. "You looked as if you'd swallowed a frog."

He stopped in the act of unlocking the passenger-side car door. "Why didn't you let *me* explain?" he asked. "She's *my* neighbor."

"She's *my* neighbor too," I pointed out. "Besides, what would you have said? At least I've been through this once before." I opened my door and got into the car. (I could see that this twin business was going to take some getting used to. Already I was noticing differences between the Dan of today and the Don of yesterday. Sure, it was only me—but I was beginning to realize that I would never be the same person twice in a row. And I would never be viewing myself through the same pair of eyes either. Dan seemed so—unsure; it was as if he was a little cowed by me. It showed in little things—his easy acquies-

44

cence of the fact that I would drive, for example. All I had
done was point him at the passenger side of the car while
I headed toward the driver's side myself, but he had
accepted it. Not without some resentment, of course; I
could see him eying me as I unlatched the top, preparatory to putting it down.)

"Put on a tape," I said, pointing at the box of cassettes.
I started to name one, then stopped. "Want me to tell
you what you're going to choose?" I realized that was a
mistake as soon as I said it.

"Uh—no, thanks," he muttered. He was frowning.

I could have kicked myself. I had let myself get carried
away with a sense of power; I hadn't been considerate of
Dan at all. Belatedly, I remembered how I had felt yesterday. Resentful, sullen, and most of all, cautious. Poor
Dan—here he was, flush with excitement, filled with a
feeling of omnipotence at the wondrous things he could
do with his timebelt—and I had stolen it all from him. By
my mere presence, my know-it-all attitude and cocksure
arrogance, I was relegating him to second fiddle. Of
course he wouldn't like it.

As he put on the tape of *Petrouchka,* I resolved to try
and be more considerate. I should have realized how he
would feel—no, that was wrong, *I did know* how he felt;
I simply hadn't paid it any mind.

Thinking back, I remembered that as Dan, my arrogance had bothered me only at first—later, as I had gotten used to the idea of "Don," I had begun to see the
wisdom of following his lead. Or had that been my reaction to Don's suddenly realized consideration of *me?*

It didn't matter. There was bound to be some confusion
at first, on both sides; what counted would be what happened later on, over dinner. I remembered how good I
had felt last night in Don's presence and I looked forward
to it again tonight; I would make it up to Dan. (The

reservations—I hadn't made them yet! No, wait a minute; it was all right. I could make the reservations any time. All I had to do was flash back a day or so; I could do it later.)

I found my way to the track easily enough; I'd been watching Don yesterday. Today Dan was watching me. Now, if I remembered correctly, there should be a parking place, right over there . . . There was, and I pulled neatly into it.

I bought a private box and had no trouble finding it. Dan was properly impressed with how well I knew my way around; actually, I was trying not to be so cocksure, but it wasn't easy. He was such a perfect audience to my self-confidence.

After we'd gotten our drinks, I remembered how Don had pretended to study the newspaper yesterday and how funny I thought that had been. So I did the same thing. I frowned and muttered thoughtfully, and Danny giggled in appreciation. Maybe he was starting to warm up to me. "I think Absolam's Ass looks pretty good in the first," I announced. "Danny, go put a hundred dollars on Absolam's Ass. To win."

He started fumbling in his pockets. I pulled out some bills from mine. "Here," I said impulsively, "Make it two hundred."

He blinked and took the two hundred-dollar bills I was holding out. "You want to get rich?" I said. "You have to risk money to make it."

He went off to place the bet, leaving me to wonder what I had done. Don had given me only one hundred dollars. I had given Dan twice as much. I had changed the past again!

First the sweater and slacks, now the amount of the first bet, yet *I remembered it happening the other way—*

46

Paradox? A pair of paradoxes? I finished my drink thoughtfully, then finished Danny's.

Absolam's Ass paid off at three to one and we had six hundred dollars. I went and got two more drinks while Danny went to bet on Fig Leaf. I found myself wondering—if I could change the past so easily, maybe it wasn't as fixed as I thought it was, maybe Fig Leaf wouldn't win this time. But on the other hand, I hadn't done anything that would have any effect on that, had I?

Fig Leaf paid off at two to one. We now had twelve hundred dollars. I had another drink.

Calamity Jane came in on schedule too. We doubled our money again.

The next race was the fun one. I'd forgotten about Harass bumping Tumbleweed. When Finders Keepers came in second, Dan looked at me in confusion. "Wait—" I grinned. After Harass was disqualified, we were worth nineteen thousand, two hundred dollars. I felt great. We could keep this up all afternoon and we would end up with $750,000—no, twice that; I had doubled our original bet. We'd take home a million and a half! "Go put it all on Big John," I said. I must have been getting a little dreamy.

Dan went off, but almost immediately, he was back. No—I stood up in surprise—this was *Don*. "What are you doing here?" I asked.

"Sit down," he said. He looked grim.

"What's the matter?"

He handed me a newspaper. It looked like today's *Herald-Examiner*. I opened it up—

The headline glared: IDENTICAL TWINS TAKE TRACK FOR $1,500,000! And in smaller type: *Track Officials Promise Investigation.*

I looked at Don. Confused.

He looked back. Angry. "Don't be greedy," he said. "Quit before it gets too big."

"I don't understand—" I started to stammer.

"I've come from the middle of next week," he whispered. "Only in that future, we're in trouble. *Big* trouble. We won too much money here at the track today, so I've come back to tell you not to win any more. Else they'll get suspicious."

"How about one more bet?" I asked. "Michelangelo will make us worth a hundred and fifteen thousand, two hundred dollars."

He frowned. "Even that might be too much." His eyes blazed; he gripped my arm. "Dan, listen to me—you don't want publicity! None at all! Don't let them take any pictures and don't talk to reporters." He looked at his watch. "Dan will be back any minute. I've got to go. Read the newspaper if you have any doubts—" Then he left. I watched him as he strode away, then I looked at the *Examiner*. The story was pretty ugly. I just managed to fold it up and shove it under the seat when Dan returned.

He started to ask something about the next race, but I cut him off. "Don't worry about it. We're leaving right after this. We're through for the day."

"Huh—? Why?"

I waited till after the horses broke from the gate. Sure enough, Big John broke first to take an early lead. I said, "Because in a few minutes we're going to be worth fifty-seven thousand, six hundred dollars. Don't you think that's enough?"

"But if we keep going," he protested, "we can make a million and a half dollars on an eight-horse parlay."

I winced. I thought of the newspaper under my seat. "There are better ways to make a million and a half dollars," I said. "Quieter ways, more discreet."

He didn't answer. I waited till Big John crossed the

finish line and paid off at three to one. I scooped up my newspapers and stood. "Come on," I said. "You go get the money. I'll wait for you at the car."

I think he wanted me to go with him, but I had to be alone for a while. I had a lot to think about and I was suddenly in a very, very bad mood.

Oh, it wasn't the money—I'd already realized that if I could make fifty-seven thousand, six hundred dollars in one day at the races, I could easily turn that into more in the stock market. And there were other ways I could make a fortune too—

No, it wasn't the money. It was the implications of the visit from Don.

This Don, the new one, the one who had given me the newspaper—where had *he* come from? The future obviously, but *which* future? His world was one that no longer existed—no, never would exist. We were leaving the races without taking the track for a million and a half dollars.

I reached the car and got in on the passenger side. I didn't feel like driving back. I started to toss the papers into the back seat, then stopped. I looked at them again. One had a small story on page one: FIVE-HORSE PARLAY WINS $57,600! The other: IDENTICAL TWINS TAKE TRACK FOR $1,500,000! A banner headline.

Both newspapers were dated the same, yet they were from two different alternate worlds.

The $57,600-world was mine; I knew the events in it because I had lived them. The $1,500,000-world was Don's, but he had talked me out of the actions that would eventually produce his future.

Where had that future gone? Where had Don gone? Had they both ceased to exist?

No. I still had the newspaper. That proved something. Or did it?

I had the paper in my hands—it was real. But you couldn't take it back—I mean, forward—to the future it came from because that future no longer existed. Shouldn't the newspaper cease to exist too?

The "Don" who had come back in time to talk me out of the actions that had produced the time he had come from—what had happened to him?

Where was he now?

If he stayed here—like the newspaper—he wouldn't disappear. (Were there *actually* two of me now?) But on the other hand, if he bounced forward from *now*, he'd only arrive in *this* world's future, so he wouldn't disappear that way either. He wouldn't disappear unless he could get back to his own future, and that didn't exist, so he couldn't do that—

Was he waiting for me in tomorrow?

No. The whole thing didn't make sense. It didn't seem logical that every time I went back and talked myself out of an action that I would duplicate myself—

But it seemed the only answer. Every time I changed the past, I was creating an alternate world—

Now, wait a minute—I had already changed the past! I had worn different clothes and I had given Dan two hundred dollars to bet instead of one hundred. And the newspaper I had brought with me—

The newspaper, of course! It had been staring at me all the time. FIVE-HORSE PARLAY WINS $57,600!

But it wasn't a five-horse parlay—not any more! It was only a four-horse parlay; we hadn't stayed to bet on Michelangelo. We'd doubled the first bet; it was only coincidence that we'd ended up with the same amount.

But the important thing was: *I had changed the past.* Just as Don had come back in time to change his past, so I had done the same thing to my past, though not on as large a scale. I remembered my past differently—I remembered different clothes, a different bet and a five-horse parlay. I remembered it the way it had happened to me, but I had changed it.

Now, where was *my* Don—the one I had gone to the races with? Where was he?

The situation was exactly the same: I had changed the past and destroyed his future. So where was he?

Well, that was silly. He was *me*. He hadn't disappeared —he was right here. I had simply done things differently this time around.

Hmm.

That meant that the Don who had come back in time with the newspaper was *me* too. (Of course—but would *I* have to go back in time to warn myself? No, because I hadn't let the bets go that far.)

Then, if he was *me* . . . there really was only *one* of me! He would go back to the future—*my* future, *our* future—with his memories, but—

But if his memories were different from mine, how could we be the same person?

(And where was the Don *I* had gone to the races with? The one who had worn a sweater and slacks and bet only a hundred dollars?)

Danny showed up then, he was giddy and excited— like he'd invented money. He waved the check at me. "You want to see it?"

I took it thoughtfully and looked. I took *my* check out of my pocket and compared them—they were *not* identical. The check number on Danny's was lower and the signatures were not quite the same.

Of course, how could they be identical? We were leaving earlier in the day after a different set of bets. The situations were not the same—why should the checks be?

Then, this check I was carrying—it was no longer any good, it was from a world that no longer existed.

And it was the same situation with the disappearing Don; he was a canceled check in this world, wasn't he?

But the canceled check *hadn't* disappeared. I still had it.

(I remembered myself asking if we could cash them both.)

I'd been fooled once by the illusion of the duplicated check, but this time the check *had been* duplicated!

And if I could duplicate the check, then couldn't I have duplicated myself?

There was another side to it too.

I'd already eliminated two possible futures: the one where I'd worn slacks and a sweater and the one where I'd won a million and a half dollars.

As far as I knew, both of those Dons had ceased to exist along with their futures. Neither seemed to be still around.

And if I could eliminate *them*—

—what was to keep some other Dan from eliminating me?

Perhaps even now—

*　　*　　*

No. There must be something I was misunderstanding.

Danny drove. He babbled incessantly; he was like a schoolgirl. But I wasn't listening anyway. I was too pre-occupied with my own thoughts.

I knew there was an answer.

There *had* to be.

For one thing, paradoxes were supposed to be impossible.

Oh, sure, I know—time travel makes the most horrendous of paradoxes possible, even probable; but that's just not so. A paradox would be a violation of the laws of nature, and there's just no way to violate the laws of nature. *By definition,* they're the laws of nature. And inviolable.

Hence, paradoxes are impossible.

If paradoxes were possible, then time travel would have to be impossible—otherwise, we'd have people killing their grandfathers right and left. We'd have people seducing their mothers or kidnaping their fathers. We'd have time travelers killing the inventors of time machines. We'd have all manner of anachronisms and flukes, and the laws of nature would be violated in a hundred different ways.

But time travel *was* possible. I had proved it myself. So paradoxes were *impossible.*

It sounded all very neat when I explained it to myself that way. Paradoxes had to be impossible; therefore, they were. Everything could be worked out logically—

Then, dammit, why couldn't I work this one out? If this wasn't a paradox, it was still way ahead of whatever was in second place.

* * *

All right. Let's assume that paradoxes are impossible—then where do I go from here?

The checks, for instance. Obviously, Danny's check was the good one, the one we would have to cash in order to collect our winnings. But the question was *how?*

Should I take it forward with me into the future? But then what would Danny have to show himself when he was Don? (Of course, I hadn't made a *point* of comparing the checks this time around, had I?) But if I left it here in the past, how would I get it in the future?

My check shouldn't exist. It was from a canceled world. Danny's check was the only valid one here because I had done things differently from the way they had originally occurred. If I had done things the way Don had done, I would have had the "duplicate" of Danny's check.

But I hadn't. I had tampered with the timestream and didn't have a valid check at all. And that meant—

—that I was in an unstable situation.

Because whatever I did now, this Danny—when he became Don and went back in time—would *not* do exactly the same as me. It would be impossible for him to do so. Just as I had eliminated the Don preceding me, this Danny was going to eliminate the Don preceding him —*me!*

No, that wasn't right; I was thinking in paradoxes again. After all, I was here and alive—I was *me*. I hadn't eliminated Don at all. I had become him and done things differently, that's all. (But then what had become of the Don who had done things the other way? And what had become of the Don who had given me the newspaper and told me not to be so greedy? Forget about *them*— you simply won't become them, that's all.)

Let's see . . . there must be a way to figure this out.

Danny had to go back in time and become Don to his Dan.

If he takes his check back with him, I won't have it to cash. On the other hand, if I take it forward with me, he won't have a check to show his Danny. (He'll be changing the timestream, just like me. Unless—)

What if I gave Danny the false check to take back with him?

My mind began to boggle.

But it *was* the answer, of course. *This* Danny would

become *my* Don! That's why his check would match mine
when he went back to meet me—(and he'd test to see if
he could change the past too! He'd try wearing different
clothes than me: the slacks and sweater!)

And I'd still end up with the money!

Yes, of course. It had to be the answer.

I'd been sitting and staring at the checks for the past
ten miles. Now I handed Danny the false one and he
slipped it into his pocket without even looking at it. (Ha-
ha! I cackled gleefully to myself.)

I realized Danny was saying something: "—what happens now? Do you go back to your time?"

I grinned at him. "Not yet. First we go out to celebrate.
Like rich people."

This time I won the argument over who was going to
use the bathroom first. I don't mind sharing my razor, but
at least I ought to get first shave off the new blade. Danny
seemed a little bothered by the pseudo-intimacy of both
of us dressing out of the same closet, so I compromised
and let him wear the red sport jacket. While he showered,
I reset my belt and flipped back to morning, phoned *The*
Restaurant and made reservations for two, then flashed
forward again, appearing at the exact instant I had disappeared and in the same spot. The air hadn't even had
time to rush in. (That was one way to minimize the jump-
shock.)

It was at *The* Restaurant that I began to realize what
Don had meant the night before and why he had said
what he did. Danny looked so . . . innocent. So unpro-
tected. He *needed* someone. And I could be that someone—I *was* that someone; I knew Danny better than
anyone.

He was my "little brother"—I would have to watch out
for him; and that would make him feel as secure as I felt

when *my* "big brother" Don was around. It was a strange feeling—exciting.

"You'll never have to be alone again," I told him. (I knew how lonely he was; I knew how much he hated it.) "You'll always have me. I'll always have you. It makes more sense this way." (I would keep him from falling into those bitter, empty moods, those gritty moments of aching frustration. It would be good for *both* of us.) "I don't like being alone either. This way I can share the things I like with somebody I know likes them too." (No, I would never be lonely again; I would have my Danny to take care of. And my Don to take care of me. Oh, it was such a wonderful feeling to have—how could I make him see?) "I don't have to try and impress you, you don't have to impress me. There's perfect understanding, there'll never be any of those destructive little head games that people play on each other, because we're a perfect match." It all came spilling out, a flood of emotion. (I wanted to reach out and touch him. I wanted to hold him.) "I like *me*, Danny; that's why I like *you*. You'll feel the same way, you'll see.

"And I guarantee, there are no two people in this world who understand each other as well as we do."

* * *

Life is full of little surprises.

Time travel is full of big ones.

My worrying about paradoxes and canceled checks had been needless. If I had thought to read the timebelt instructions completely before I went gallivanting off to the past and the future, I would have known.

I was right that paradoxes were impossible, but I was

wrong in thinking that the timestream had to be protected from them. After all, they were impossible. It wouldn't have mattered whether I had given Danny a check or not; changes in the timestream are cumulative, not variable.

What this means is that you can change the past as many times as you want. You can't eliminate *yourself*.

I could go back in time nineteen years and strangle myself in my crib, but *I* wouldn't cease to exist. (I'd have a dead baby on my hands though . . .)

Look, you can change the future, right? The future is exactly the same as the past, only it hasn't happened yet. *You* haven't perceived it. The real difference between the two—the *only* difference—is *your* point of view. If the future can be altered, so can the past.

Every change you make is cumulative; it goes on top of every other change you've already made, and every change you add later will go on top of that. You can go back in time and talk yourself out of winning a million and a half dollars, but the resultant world is *not* one where you didn't win a million and a half dollars; it's a world where you talked yourself out of it. See the difference?

It's slight—but it's important.

Think of an artist drawing a picture. But he's using indelible ink and he doesn't have an eraser. If he wants to make a change, he has to paint over a line with white. The line hasn't ceased to exist; it's just been painted over and a new line drawn on top.

On the surface, it doesn't seem to make much difference. The finished picture will look the same whether the artist uses an eraser or a gallon of white paint, but it is important to the artist. *He's* aware of the process he used to obtain the final result, and it affects his consciousness. He's aware of all the lines and drawings beneath the final one, the layer upon layer of images, each one not quite the one—all those discarded pieces; they haven't ceased to exist, they've just been painted out of view.

Subjectively, time travel is like that.

I can lay down one timeline and then go back and do things differently the second time around. I can go back a third time and talk myself out of something, and I can go back a fourth time and change it still again. And in the end, the timestream is exactly what I've made it—it is the cumulative product of my changes. The closest I can get to the original is to go back and talk myself out of something. It won't be the *same* world, but the difference will be undetectable. The difference will be in *me*. I—like the artist with his painting—will be conscious of all the other alternatives that did exist, do exist, and can exist again.

A world where I did not win a million and a half dollars is not the same as a world where I talked myself out of winning a million and a half dollars. The difference is Daniel Eakins.

My memories are other than what they would be, so is my awareness. I am the result of the cumulative changes in my timestream. My thoughts will be altered by this awareness, and so will my actions.

The world I came from is like my innocence. I can never recapture it. At best, I can only simulate it.

You can't be a virgin twice.

(Not that I would, of course. Virginity seems like a nice state of existence only to a virgin, only to someone who doesn't know any better. From this side of the fence, it seems like such a waste. I remember my first time, and how I had reacted: Why, this was nothing to be scared of at all—in fact, it's wonderful! Why had I taken so long to discover it? Afterward, all the time beforehand looked so . . . empty.)

According to the timebelt instructions, what I had done by altering the situation the second time around was called *tangling*. Mine had been a simple tangle, easily unraveled, but there was no limit to how complex a tangle could be. You can tie as many knots in a ball of yarn as you like.

There really isn't any reason to unravel tangles (according to the instructions) because they usually take care of themselves; but the special cautions advise against letting a tangle get too complex because of the cumulative effects that might occur. You might suddenly find that you've changed your world beyond all recognition—and possibly beyond your ability to *excise.*

Excising is what you do when you bounce back and talk yourself out of something—when you go back and undo a mistake. Like winning too much at the races. (How about that? I'd been tangling and excising and I hadn't even known it.)

The belt explained the impossibility of paradoxes this way: if there was only *one* timestream, then paradoxes would be possible and time travel would have to be impossible. But every time you make a change in the timestream, no matter how slight, you are creating *another* timestream. (As far as you are concerned, it is the only timestream, because you can't get back to the first one.)

So when you use the timebelt, you aren't really jumping through time, that's an illusion; what you are doing is leaving one timestream and jumping to—no, *creating* —another. The second one is identical to the one you have left, including all of the changes you have made in it— *up to the instant of your appearance.* At that moment you have changed the second timestream into a *different* timestream. Your mere existence in it is a change.

If you travel back in time to excise an action, you are creating that second universe at an earlier moment, but it will develop in exactly the same direction as the universe you just left, *unless* you take direct steps to alter that development.

That the process is perceived as time travel is only an illusion, because the process is subjective. But because it's subjective, it really doesn't make any difference. It's just as good as the real thing. Better, even; because nothing is permanent; nothing is irrevocable.

The past is the future. The future is the past. There's no difference between the two and either can be changed. I'm flashing across a series of alternate worlds, creating and destroying a new one every time I bounce.

The universe is infinite.

And so are the possibilities of my life.

*   *   *

I am Dan. And I am Don.

And sometimes I am Dean, and Dino, and Dion, and Dana. And more . . .

There's a poker game going on in my apartment. It starts on June 24, 1975. I don't know when it ends. Every time one of me gets tired, there's another one showing up to take his place. The game is a twenty-four-hour marathon. I know it lasts at least a week; on July 2 I peeked in and saw several versions of myself—some in their mid-twenties—still grimly playing.

Okay. So I like poker.

Every time I'm in the mood, I know where there's an empty chair. And when. Congenial people too. I know they'll never cheat.

I may have to get a larger apartment though. Five

rooms is not enough. (I need more room for the pool table.)

Strange things keep happening—no, not strange things, things that I've learned not to question. For instance, once I saw Uncle Jim—he looked surprised and vanished almost immediately; it startled me too. I was just getting used to the idea of his death. I hadn't realized that he would have been using the timebelt too. (But why not?)

Another time I heard strange noises from the bedroom. When I peeked in, there was Don in bed with—well, whoever it was, she was covered by a blanket, I couldn't see. He just looked at me with a silly expression, not the slightest bit embarrassed, so I shrugged and closed the door. And the noises began again.

I'm not questioning it at all. I'll find out. Eventually.

Mostly I've been concentrating on making money. Don and I (and later, Danny and I) have made a number of excursions into the past, as well as the future. Some of our investments go back as far as 1850 (railroads, coal, steel). 1875 (Bell Telephone). 1905 (automobiles, rubber, oil, motion pictures). 1910 (airlines, heavy industry, steel again). 1920 (radio, insurance companies, chemicals, drugs). 1929 (I picked up some real bargains here. More steel. Business machines. More radio, more airlines. More automobiles). 1940 (companies that would someday be involved in computers, television, and the aerospace industry).

Down through the decades, I bought a little here, a little there—not enough to change the shape of the world, but enough to supply me with a lifetime comfortable fortune. It was a little tricky setting up an investment firm to manage it, but it was worth the effort. When I got back to 1975, I found I was worth—

—one hundred and forty-three million dollars.

Hmm.

Actually, that number was meaningless. I was worth a hell of a lot more. It turned out I owned an investment monopoly worth several billion dollars, or let's say I controlled it. What I owned was the holding company that held the holding companies. By the numbers, its value was only one hundred and forty-three million, but I could put my hands on a lot more than that if I wanted.

What it meant was that I had unlimited credit.

Hell! If I wanted to, I could *own* the country! The world!

Believe it or not, I didn't want to.

I'd lost interest in the money. It was just so much numbers. Useless except as a tool to manipulate my environment, and I had a much *better* tool for that.

Those frequent trips to the past had whetted my appetite. I had seen New York grow—like a living creature, the city had swelled and soared; her cast-iron façades had become concrete; her marble towers gave way to glass-sided slabs and soaring monoliths. I became intrigued with history—

I went back to see the burning of the *Hindenburg*. I was there when the great Zeppelin shriveled in flame and an excited announcer babbled into his microphone.

I was there when Lindbergh took off and I was there when he landed.

I was there when an airplane smacked into the Empire State Building, shattering glass and concrete and tumbling to the horrified streets below. It was unreal.

I saw the Wright brothers' first flight. That was unreal too.

And I know what happened to Judge Crater.

I saw the blast-off of Apollo 11. It was the loudest sound I've ever heard.

And I witnessed the assassination of Abraham Lincoln. It wasn't dramatic at all; it was sad and clumsy.

62

I was there (via timeskim) at Custer's last stand.

I witnessed the completion of the first transcontinental railroad. (The guy who was supposed to pound in the gold spike slipped and fell in the mud.)

I've seen the Chicago fire and the San Francisco earthquake.

I was at the signing of the Declaration of Independence. (How far we have come since then . . .)

I saw the burning of Atlanta.

And I've seen the original uncut version of D.W. Griffith's *Intolerance* and Merian C. Cooper's *King Kong*.

I was there the day the Liberty Bell cracked.

And I saw the fall of the Alamo.

I witnessed the battle of the *Monitor* and the *Merrimac*.

I attended a band concert of John Philip Sousa.

I heard Lincoln deliver his Gettysburg Address. I recorded it on tape.

I've seen Paul Revere's midnight ride and the Boston Tea Party.

I've met George Washington and Thomas Jefferson.

And I watched Columbus come ashore.

I saw Ben Franklin flying a kite on a rainy day.

I was there when Bell tested his first telephone. "Mr. Watson, come here. I want you."

I witnessed Galileo's experiment—when he dropped two lead balls of different weights from the tower of Pisa.

I have seen performances of plays by William Shakespeare. At the Globe Theatre in London.

I watched Leonardo da Vinci as he painted the "Mona Lisa." (I will not tell you why she smiles.) And I watched as his rival, Michelangelo, painted the Sistine Chapel.

I've heard Strauss waltzes, conducted by Strauss himself.

I was at the disastrous premier of Stravinsky's *Rite of Spring*. And Ravel's *Bolero* too.

I've heard Beethoven's symphonies—as conducted by Beethoven himself.

And Mozart. And Bach. (I've seen the Beatles too.)

And the beheading of Ann Boleyn. And Thomas More.

I've seen the signing of the Magna Charta.

I have visited Imperial Rome. Nero and Tiberius and Julius Caesar himself. Cleopatra was ugly.

And ancient Greece. The sacking of Troy was more than a myth.

I have witnessed performances of plays by Sophocles and watched as Plato taught Aristotle and Aristotle taught Alexander. I watched as Socrates drank hemlock.

I have witnessed the crucifixion of one Jesus Christ of Nazareth.

And more.

I have seen dinosaurs. I have seen the thunder lizards walk the Earth. The *Brontosaurus*, the *Stegosaurus*, and *Triceratops*—and the *Tyrannosaurus Rex*, the most fearsome monster ever to stalk the world.

I have seen the eruption of Vesuvius and the death of Pompeii.

I have seen the explosion of Krakatoa.

I watched an asteroid plunge from the sky and shatter a giant crater in what would someday be Arizona.

I've witnessed the death of Hiroshima by atomic fire.

I've timeskimmed from the far distant past and watched as the Colorado River carved out the Grand Canyon—a living, twisting snake of water cutting away the rock.

And more.

I've been to the year 2001. I've been to the moon.

I've walked its surface in a flimsy spacesuit and held its

dust in my hands. I've seen the Earth rise above the Lunar Apennines.

I've visited Tranquillity Base—and flashing back to the past, I watched the *Eagle* land. I saw Neil Armstrong come ashore.

And more.

I've been to Mars. I've been to the great hotels that orbit Jupiter, and I've seen the rings of Saturn.

I've timeskimmed from the far past to the far future.

I have seen Creation.

And I have seen Entropy.

From Great Bang to Great Bang—the existence of the Earth is less than a blink; the death of the sun by nova, almost unnoticeable.

I've seen the future of mankind—

I like to think I understand, but I know that I don't. The future of the human race is as alien and incomprehensible to me as the year 1975 would be to a man of Napoleon's era. But wondrous it is indeed, and filled with marvelous things.

There is nothing that I cannot witness—

—but there is little that I can participate in.

I am limited. By my language, by my appearance, by my skin color, and my height.

I am limited to life in a span of history maybe two hundred years in each direction. Beyond that, the languages are difficult: the meanings have altered, the pronunciations and usages too complex to decipher. With effort, perhaps, I can communicate; but the farther I go from 1975, the harder it is to make myself understood.

And there are other differences. In the past, I am too tall. The farther back I travel, the shorter is the human race. In the future, I am too short—mankind's evolution is upward.

And there are still *other* differences. *Disturbing* ones.

There are places where my skin is the wrong color, or my eyes the wrong shape. And there is one time in the future when I am the wrong sex.

There are places where people's faces are—different.

I can witness.

I cannot participate.

But witnessing is enough: I have seen more of history than any other human being. I have timeskimmed and timestopped and my journeys have been voyages of mystery and adventure.

There is much that I don't understand. There are things that are incomprehensible to one who is not of the era and the culture.

But still—the proper study of man is man himself.

History is more than just old gossip.

It's majesty. It's pomp and circumstance. It's the blare of trumpets and the stamp of boots; the sudden cry, the smell of fear—confusion, panic, disaster—

—and above all, *triumph!* The triumph of man over his environment; the continual victory of the intellect over the animal; the unquenchable vitality of life! Sometimes seething, sometimes dirty, sometimes unspeakably evil.

But always the direction is upward.

If I must taste a bitterness, it is worth it; because I have shared the dreams.

And the promise.

I have seen its fulfillment.

I know the truth and the destiny of the human race.

It is a proud and lonely thing to be a man.

* * *

This part, I think, may be the hardest to record.

It was inevitable, I suppose, that it happened, but it

has caused me to do some serious thinking. About myself. About Dan. About Don.

When Uncle Jim died, I thought my life would be changed, and I worried about the directions it might take. When I thought I had eliminated myself by a time-belt paradox, I realized how much I feared dying—I realized how much I needed to be Dan to my Don and Don to my Dan.

But this—

—this makes me question the shape of my whole life. What am I? Who am I?

What am I doing to myself?

Have I made a wrong decision? Am I moving in a strange and terrible direction?

I wish I knew.

It started—when? yesterday evening? Time is funny when you don't live it linearly. When I get tired, I sleep. I flip forward or backward to the nearest nighttime and climb into bed.

If I'm not tired, and it's night, I flash to day and go to the beach. Or I jump to winter and go skiing. I stay as long as I want, or as short as I want. I stay for weeks or only a few minutes. I'm not a slave to the clock—nor even to the seasons.

What I mean is, I'm no longer living in a straight line.

I bounce back and forth through the days like a temporal ping-pong ball. I don't even know how old I am any more. I think I've passed my twentieth birthday, but I'm not sure.

It's strange . . .

Time used to be a flowing river. I sailed down it and watched the shores sweep past: here, a warm summer evening, ice tinkling in lemonade glasses; there, a cool fall morning, dead leaves crunching underfoot and my breath in frosty puffs; a slowly shifting panorama. But I was only a leaf in the water. I was carried helplessly along, I was a victim of the current.

Now I'm out of the river and standing on the bank; time is no longer a moving entity to me, but a vast spread-out landscape. I can leap to any point on it at will. Do I like that summer day? Yes, here it is. Am I in the mood for a fall morning? Ah, that's nice. I don't have to wait for the river to carry me to a place where I might be able to find that moment—I can go exactly to it.

No moment can ever escape me. I've chased twilight and captured dawn. I've conquered day and tamed the night. I can live as I choose because I am the master of time.

I laugh to think of it. Time is an everlasting smorgasbord—and I am the gourmet, picking here, choosing there, discarding this unnecessary bit of tripe and taking an extra piece of filet instead.

But even this temporal mobility—no matter how unlimited it is—does not keep me from arbitrarily dividing things into "day" and "night." That is, it must be a human thing to want to divide eternity into bite-sized chunks. It's easier to digest. So no matter how many jumps I make, anything that happened before my last sleep happened "yesterday," and everything since I woke up (and until I go to sleep again) is part of my "today." Some of my "todays" have spanned a thousand years. And "tomorrow" comes not with the dawn, but with my next awakening.

(Generally, I think I'm still on a twenty-four-hour life cycle, but I can't be sure. If I add a few extra hours to my "day" so as to enjoy the beach a little longer, I find my body tends to obey the local time, not mine. Perhaps Man is unconsciously geared to the sun. At least, it seems that way. I don't get tired until after the world gets dark.)

68

(But like I said before, I'm not sure how old I am any more. I've lost track.)

Anyway. What I'm getting to is that this happened "yesterday."

Don and I were listening to Beethoven. (The *original* Beethoven. I had gotten a recorder from 2010, a multi-channel device capable of greater fidelity than anything known in 1975, and had taped all eleven of the master's symphonies. Yes. All *eleven.*)

We had spent the day swimming—skinny-dipping actually (it's strange to watch your own nude body from a distance), and now we were resting up before dinner. I have this mansion in the hills overlooking the San Fernando Valley; the view is fantastic, even the bedroom has a picture window.

It was dusk. The sun was just dipping behind the hills to the west. It was large and orange through the haze. Don had turned on the stereo and collapsed exhaustedly on the bed (a king-size water bed) without even toweling off.

I didn't think anything of it. I was tired too. I made an attempt to dry myself off, then lay down beside him. (I'd gotten into a very bad habit with Don—with Dan—with myself. I'd discovered I didn't like being alone. Even when I sleep, I need the assurance of knowing there's somebody next to me. So more and more I found myself climbing into bed with one or more versions of myself. Sometimes there's a lot of horseplay and giggling. What did I want? Did I know? Is that why I did it? It extends to other things too. I won't swim alone. And several times I've showered together, ostensibly so we could scrub each other's back.)

We were both stretched out naked on the water bed, just staring at the ceiling and listening to the Pastoral

Symphony, that part near the beginning where it goes *"pah-rump-pah-pah, rump-pah-pah . . ."* (You know, where Disney's joyous trumpets announce a cascade of happy unicorns.)

It was very relaxing. We had this giant electric hookah (1997) and we were passing the mouthpiece back and forth. It was very good grass; I was pleasantly floating, and the light show on the ceiling was swirling in red and pink and purple, shifting to blue and white.

I'd been getting strange vibrations from Don all day. I wasn't sure why. (Or perhaps I hadn't wanted to admit—) He kept looking at me. His glance kept meeting mine and he seemed to be smiling about some inner secret, but he wouldn't say what it was. He touched me a lot too. There had been a lot of clowning around in the pool, and once I thought he had been about to— (I must have sensed it earlier, I must have; but I must have been refusing to recognize it.)

The symphony had reached that point where it suggests wild dancing, with several false stops, when a soft *pop!* in the air made me look up. Another Don. I had long since gotten used to various versions of myself materializing and disappearing at random. But I sat up anyway.

He looked troubled. And tired.

"Which one of you is Dan?" he said. He looked at me. "You are, aren't you?"

I nodded.

Don, beside me, raised up on one elbow, sending ripples through the bed, but his gaze was veiled. Don II looked at him but stepped toward me. He was holding a sheaf of papers—I recognized it as my, no, *his*—diary; that is, his version of my diary.

"I want to excise something," he said.

"What?"

70

"That is, I think I want to excise it. I'm not sure—" He looked at me. He sat down on the bed, and for a moment I thought he was close to tears. He was trembling. "Look, I don't know if this—this *thing* is good or bad or what. Maybe the terms are meaningless. I just don't know. I'm not sure if I should tell you to avoid this or whether I should let you make your own decision." He looked at both of us. "I can't talk about it. I mean, I can't talk about it to *you* because you wouldn't understand. Not yet. That's why I have to do it this way. Here's my diary. Read it, Dan. Then you decide for yourself if—if that's what you want. I mean, it's the only way. You shouldn't stumble into this. You should either go into it with your eyes open and be aware of what you're doing, or you should reject it because you're aware of its possibility. Either way, it's going to change your—our—life."

He was very upset, and that made me very concerned. I reached out and touched his arm. He flinched and pulled away. "Tell me what it is—" I said.

He shook his head adamantly. "Just read the diary."

"I will," I promised. "But stay here until I do, so you can talk to me about it."

"No, I can't. I tried that once and we ended up doing exactly what I came back to stop. I mean, I mustn't be here if you're to make your own choice." And he popped out of existence. Back to his own future—my future perhaps? I won't know till I get there.

I picked up the papers and paged through them.

The early parts were identical to mine, even up to the point where Don and I were listening to Beethoven, stretched out on the water bed—

*   *   *

What I'm trying to get at is that it happened almost accidentally.

We were pleasantly floating on top of a marijuana high. The music gave it a soft glow. We passed the mouthpiece of the water pipe back and forth and watched the colors slide across the ceiling. When the pipe went out, Don leaned across me to put it on the end table, but instead of pulling back, he just sighed and stretched out next to me, one arm across my chest.

Absent-mindedly I reached up and stroked his arm. In response, he gave me a casual hug.

And then he was looking at me and our eyes were locked in another of those mysterious glances. He was all smiles. "What is it?" I asked.

In answer, he slid himself upward and kissed me.

Just a kiss. Quick, affectionate—and loaded with desire.

He pulled back and looked at me, still smiling, watching my reaction.

I was confused. Because I had *accepted* it. I had *let* him kiss me as if it were a totally natural thing for him to do. I hadn't questioned it at all. His eyes were shining, and I studied them carefully. He lowered his face to mine again . . .

This time the kiss was longer. Much longer.

And he didn't just kiss me. He slid his arms around me and pulled me to him.

And I helped.

We stretched out side by side, facing each other on the water bed. We put our arms around each other. And we kissed.

I realized I liked it.

I liked it.

"Don," I managed to gasp. "We shouldn't—"

He studied me. "But you want to, don't you?" And I knew he was right.

"Yes, but—" His face was so open, his eyes were so deep. "But it's wrong—"

"Is it? Why is it?"

"It's not right—"

"Is it any worse than masturbation? You masturbated yesterday, Danny, I know. Because I did too. You were alone in the house, but you're never alone from yourself."

"I—I—but masturbation isn't—I mean, that's—"

"Danny"—he silenced me with a finger across my lips—"I want to give you pleasure, I want to give you *me*. You have your arms around me. You have your hands on me. You like what you feel, I know you do."

And he was right. I did like it. I did enjoy it.

He was so sure of himself.

"Just relax, Danny," he whispered. "Just relax." He kissed me again and I kissed him back.

*　*　*

I've done it twice now. I've been seduced and I've seduced myself. Or maybe I should say, after Don seduced me, I seduced Danny.

I'm filled with the joy of discovery. A sense of sharing. My relations with Don—with Dan—have taken on a new *intensity*. There is a lot more touching, a lot more laughter, a lot more . . . intimacy.

I look forward to tonight—and yet, I also hold myself back. The anticipation is delightful. Tonight, tonight . . . (I begin to understand *emotion*. I know why there are love songs. I touch the button on my belt. I fly to meet myself.)

*   *   *

So this is love.

The giving. The taking.

The abandonment of roles. The opening of the self. And the resultant sensuality of it all. The delight. The laughing joy.

Were I to describe in clinical detail for some unknown reader those things that we have actually done, the intensity and pleasure would not come through. The joy would be filtered out. The written paragraphs would be grotesque. Perverse.

Because love cannot be discussed objectively.

It is a subjective thing. You must be immersed in it to understand it. The things that Danny and I (Don and I) have done, we've done them out of curiosity and delight. Not compulsion. Delight.

And joyous sexuality. We are discovering our bodies. We are discovering each other. We are children with a magnificent new toy. Yes, sex is a toy for grownups.

To describe the things we have been doing would deprive them of their special intimacy and magic. We do them because they feel good. We do them because in this way we make each other feel good. We do it out of love.

Is this love?

It must be. Why didn't I do this sooner?

*   *   *

And yet, I wonder what I am doing.

A vague sense of *wrongness* pervades my life. I find myself looking over my shoulder a lot— Who's watching me? Who's judging my days?

74

Is it wrong?

I don't know.

There is no one I can talk to about it, not even myself. Every Don I know—every Dan—is caught up in the same whirlpool. None of us is any closer to the truth. We are all confused.

I'm alone for the first time in days.

It makes no difference. I'm still talking to myself.

I wish some Don from the future would come back to advise me—but even that's a useless wish. Any Don who did come back would only be trying to shape me toward *his* goals, regardless of mine.

(I did meet one once. I don't know if it was intentional or accidental. He looked to be in his mid-thirties, maybe older; there were tiny lines at the corners of his eyes. He was a little darker and a lot heavier than me. He said, "You look troubled, Danny. Would you like to talk about it?" I said yes, but when we sat down on the couch, he put his arm around my shoulders and tried to pull me close. I fled into yesterday—Is that my future? Am I condemning myself to a life of that?)

(Is *condemning* even the right word? There are times when I am lying in Danny's arms when I am so happy I want to shout. I want to go out into the middle of the street and scream as loud as I can with the overwhelming joy of how happy I am. There are times when I am with Don that I break down and cry with happiness. We *both* cry with happiness. The emotion is too much to contain. There are times when it is very good and I am happier than I have ever been in my life. Is that condemnation?)

(Must I list all those moments which I would never excise? The times we went nude swimming on a California beach centuries before the first man came to this continent. The night when six of us, naked and giggling, discovered what an orgy *really* was. [I've been to that orgy four times now—does that mean I have to visit it twice more? I hope so.] The day we made love by the pool and discovered the magnificent effects of marijuana . . . I had not realized what pleasure could be—)

But when I think about it logically, I know that it's wrong.

Man was made to mate with woman. Man was not made to mate with man.

But does that mean man must *not* mate with man?

No matter how many arguments I marshal against it, I am still outvoted by one overwhelming argument for it.

It's pleasurable. I like it.

So I rationalize. I tell myself that it's simply a complex form of masturbation, and masturbation is all right. Ninety-five percent of the people in the world indulge in it at one time or another, and the other five percent are liars.

But this isn't simply masturbation. I know it. This is something more. I respond to Dan as if he were another person, *as if he were not myself.* I am both husband and wife, and I like both roles.

Oh my God—what have I done to myself?

What have I done?

Rationalization cannot hide the truth. How can anything that has given me such happiness leave me so unhappy?

Please. Someone. Help.

❈   ❈   ❈

I put the pages down and looked at Don. The effects of the marijuana had abruptly evaporated. "You've read this, haven't you?"

He wouldn't meet my gaze; he simply nodded.

I narrowed my eyes in sudden suspicion. "How far ahead of me are you?" I asked. "One day? Two days? A week? How much of my future do you know?"

He shook his head. "Not much. A little less than a day."

"I'm your yesterday?"

He nodded.

"You know what we were about to do?" I held up the papers meaningfully.

He nodded again.

"We would have done it if he hadn't stopped us, wouldn't we?"

"Yes," said Don. "In fact, I was just about to—" He stopped, refused to finish the sentence.

I thought about that for a moment. "Then you know if we are going to—I mean, you know if we did it."

He said, "I know." His voice was almost a whisper.

Something about the way he said it made me look at him. "We did—didn't we?"

"Yes."

Abruptly, I was finding it hard to talk. He tried to look at me, but I wouldn't meet his gaze.

"Dan," he said. "You don't understand. You won't understand until you're me."

"We don't have to do it," I said. "Both of us have free will. Either of us can change the future. I could say no. And you—even though you have your memory of doing it, you could still refuse to do it again. You could change the past. If you wanted to."

He stretched out a hand. "It's up to you . . ."

"No," I shook my head. "You're the one who makes the decisions. *I'm* Danny, you're Don. Besides, you've already—you've already done it. You know what it's like. You know if it will . . . be good, or if we should . . . avoid it. I don't know, Don; that's why I have to trust you." I looked at him. "Do we do it?"

Hesitation. He touched my arm. "You want to, don't you?"

After a moment I nodded. "Yes. I want to see what it's like. I—I love you."

"I want to do it too."

"Is it all right, though?" I held my voice low. "I mean, remember how troubled that Don looked?"

"Danny, all I remember is how happy we were."

I looked at him. There was a tear shining on his cheek.

It was enough. I pressed against him. And we both held on tight.

* * *

I put the papers down and looked at Don. "I had a feeling we were heading toward it," I said.

He nodded. "Yes." And then he smiled. "At least, now it's out in the open."

I met his gaze. "I'm surprised it didn't happen sooner . . ."

"Think about it," he said. "It can't happen until *Danny* is ready. Any Don can try to seduce him, but unless Danny wants it to, it won't happen."

"So it's really me who's doing the seducing, isn't it?"

Don grinned. He rolled over on his back and spread his arms in invitation. "I'm ready."

So was I. I moved into them and kissed him.

And wondered why previous versions of myself had been so afraid.

I wanted to do it. Wasn't that reason enough?

* * *

Evolution, of course.

I had provided a hostile environment for those of me with doubts about their sexuality. They had excised themselves out of existence.

Leaving only me. With no doubts at all.

Survival of the fittest?

I know who I am. I know what I want.

And I'm very happy.

If I'm not, I know what I can do about it.

As I was going up the stair,
I met a man who wasn't there.
He wasn't there again today.
I wish, I wish he'd go away!

—Hughes Mearns
The Psychoed

* * *

—only, the little man was me.

I keep running into versions of myself who have come back from the future to tell me to be sure to do something or not to do something. Like, do not fly American Airlines Flight 32 from Los Angeles to New York on such and such a date. (It gets hijacked.) Or do not go faster than seventy miles per hour on the freeway today. (The highway patrol is having radar checks.) Things like that.

I used to wonder about all those other Dans and Dons—even though I knew they weren't, it still seemed like they were eliminating themselves. They're not, but it *seems* that way.

What it is, of course, is that *I* am the cumulative effect of all their changes. I—that is, *my* consciousness—have never gone back to excise anything. At least I have no memory of ever having done so. (If they didn't exist to warn me, then I wouldn't have been warned; I would have made the mistake they would have warned me against, realized it was a mistake and gone back to warn myself. Hence, *I* am the result of an inevitable sequence of variables and choices. But that precludes the concept of free will. And everything I do proves again and again that I have the ultimate free will—I don't have to be responsible for any of my actions because I can erase them any time. *But* does that erasure of certain choices always lead to a particular one, or is it just that that particular one is the one most suitable for *this* version of me? Is it my destiny to be homosexual . . . ?)

The real test of it, I guess, would be to try and excise some little incident and see what happens—see what happens to *me*. If it turns out I can remember excising it, then that'll prove I have free will.

If not—if I find I've talked myself out of something else—then I'm running along a rut, like a clockwork mechanism, doomed to play out my programmed actions for some unseen cosmic audience, and all the time believing that I have some control over those actions.

The test—

* * *

—was simple. And I passed it.

I simply went back to May 21, 1975, and talked myself out of going to the races. ("Here's today's paper," I said. "Go to the races yesterday." Danny was startled, of course, and he must have thought me a little crazy, but he agreed not to go to the races on May 21.)

So. I had excised my first trip to the track. In *this* world I hadn't made it at all.

Just to double-check, I drove out to the race track. Right. I wasn't there. (An interesting thing happened though. In the fourth race, Harass *didn't* bump Tumbleweed and wasn't disqualified. If I had been there to bet,

I would have lost everything—or would I? The Don I might have been might have foreseen that too. But why had that part of the past been changed? What had happened? Something I must have done on one of my other trips back must have affected the race.)

But I'd proved it to my own satisfaction. I had free will.

I had all of my memories of the past the way I had lived it, yet I had excised part of it out of existence. I hadn't eliminated myself and I hadn't had any of my memory magically erased. *I remembered the act of excising*.

There might have been differences—perhaps even *should have been* differences—in my world when I flashed forward again. Perhaps the mansion should have disappeared, or perhaps my fortune should have been larger or smaller; but both were unchanged. If there were any differences, they would have to be minor. I didn't go looking for them.

The reason?

The mansion had been built in 1968, a good seven years before Danny had been given the timebelt. (I had done that on purpose.) Because it had already existed in 1975, it was beyond his reach to undo unless he went back to 1967. The same applied to my financial empire; hopefully, it was beyond the reach of any casual changes.

Of course, from a *subjective* point of view, neither the mansion nor the money existed until *after* I'd gotten the timebelt—but time travel is only subjective to the traveler, not the timestream. Each time I'd made a change in the timestream, it was like a new layer to the painting. The whole thing was affected. Any change made before May 21, 1975, would be a part of Danny's world when he got the timebelt. Unless he—later on—went back and excised it in a later version of the timestream. And if he did, it still wouldn't affect me at all. It would be *his* version of the timestream and he would be a different person from me, with different memories and different desires. Just as there were alternate universes, there were also alternate Dannys.

My house already existed. My investments in the past were also firmly in existence. He could not erase them by refusing to initiate them, he would only be creating a new timestream of his own, one that would be separate from mine.

In effect, by altering my personal past, I am excising a piece of it, but I'm not destroying the continuity of this timestream. I'm only destroying my *own* continuity—except that I'm not, because I still have my memories.

Confusing? Yes, I have to keep reminding myself not to think in terms of only one timestream. I am *not* traveling in time. I am creating new universes. Alternate universes—each one identical to the one I just left up to the moment of my insertion into it. From that instant on, my existence in it causes it to take a new shape. A shape I can choose—in fact, I *must* choose; because the timestream will be changed merely by my sudden presence in it, I must make every effort to exercise control in order to prevent known sequences of events from becoming *unknown* sequences.

This applies to my own life too. I am not one person. I am many people, all stemming from the same root. Some of the other Dans and Dons I meet are greatly variant from me, others are identical. Some will repeat actions that I have done, and I will repeat the actions of others. We perceive this as a doubling back of our subjective timelines. It doesn't matter, I am me, I react to the doubling back.

From this, I've learned two things.

The first is that I do have free will.

With all that implies. If I am a homosexual, then I am that way by choice. Should that please me to know that? Or should it disturb me? I don't know—I'm the me who liked it too much to excise.

And that's the second thing I've learned—that *every* time I travel into the past, I am *excising*. I am erasing the past that was and creating a new one instead. I didn't need to excise my first trip to the races to prove that I had free will—I'd already proved it the first time I was Don, when I'd worn a windbreaker instead of a sweater.

Every time I excise, I'm not erasing a world. I'm only creating a new one for myself.

For myself—meaning, *this* me.

Because every time I excise, I am also creating versions that are not me.

There are Daniel Eakinses who are totally different people than I am.

The Danny that I told not to go to the races—he'll go off into a timestream of his own creation; he'll have different memories, and eventually, different needs and desires. His resultant timestreams may be similar to mine, but more likely, they'll be different.

And if he can be different from me—

—then there are an infinite number of Dannys who are different from me.

Somewhere there exist all the possible variations of all the possible people I could be.

I could be *any* of them—but I cannot be all.

I can only be one of the variations. I will be the variation of myself that pleases me the most.

And that suggests—

—that my free will may be only an illusion.

If there are an infinite number of Dans, then each one thinks he is choosing his own course. But that isn't so. Each one is only playing out his preordained instructions—excising, altering, and designing his timestream to fit his psychological template and following his emotional programming to its illogical extreme . . .

*   *   *

But if each of us is happiest in the universe he builds for himself, does it matter?

Does it really matter if there's no such thing as free will?

*   *   *

It bothers me—*this* me.

I need to know that there is some important reason for my existence. There must be something special about *me*.

There must be.

*   *   *

I *will* find the answer!

*   *   *

Yes. Of course.

*   *   *

I *know* what my mission is. I know who I am.

I should have realized it when the timebelt was first given to me.

I am destined to rule the universe.

I am God.

❋   ❋   ❋

But I must never let *them* find out, or they will try to kill me.

❋   ❋   ❋

I think I will kill them first.

❋   ❋   ❋

If I ever get out of this room, I will kill them all!

❋   ❋   ❋

I made a point of cautioning Danny, "Until he's cured, we'll have to be very careful to see that he doesn't get out. A paranoid schizophrenic running amok through time could be disastrous—not only for the rest of the world, but for us as well."

Danny was thoughtful as he peered through the one-way glass. "It's lucky that we caught him in time." His voice caught on the last word. I think—I *know*—he was a little shaken at seeing the drooling maniac he might have become. I hadn't gotten used to the sight either.

I said, "I think he wanted to be caught. We got him at a point where he was still conscious of what was happening to himself."

"If he ever does get his hands on another timebelt," Danny asked, "he could come back and rescue himself, couldn't he?"

I nodded. "That's partly why it was so hard to trap him. We had to get him into a timeline where he had no foreknowledge of where he was going, otherwise he would have jumped ahead to help himself against us. We wouldn't even have known about him if he hadn't kept coming farther and farther back into the past; one of us must have eventually recognized what was happening and gone for treatment, then come after this one who was still rampaging around. That's when I was called in to help. We had to deny him any chance to look into his own future until we could get the belt off him. The fact that he hasn't been rescued yet is a pretty sure indicator that he's going to be cured."

Danny grinned. "Well, just the fact that we're standing here talking about it proves that."

"Uh-uh," I said. I put my hand on his shoulder. "I'm from a line where they caught it in me before it got this far. I never went through *that*." I pointed at the glass. "You, you're a variant too. You're from even earlier. Neither of *us* is in there. He could be incurable—and if that's the case, then he has to stay in there. Forever. He has to be either completely safe, or time travel must be impossible for him. The consequences—" I didn't have to finish the sentence.

Danny bit his lip. "You're right, of course. It's just that I don't like seeing him there."

"It's for his own good," I said. "More important, it's for *our* good. If time travel is the ultimate personal freedom, then it's also the ultimate personal responsibility."

"I guess so," he said and turned away from the glass.

I didn't add anything to that and we left the hospital for the last time.

* * *

Today President Robert F. Kennedy announced that "in response to recent discoveries, the United States is initiating a high-priority research program to investigate the possibilities of travel through time."

So in order to protect my one-man monopoly, I had to go back and unkill Sirhan Sirhan.

The "recent discoveries" he was referring to were some unfortunate anachronisms which I seem to have left in the past.

I thought I had been more careful, but apparently I haven't. One of the Pompeiian artifacts in the British Museum has definitely been identified as a fossilized Coca-Cola bottle from the Atlanta, Georgia, bottling plant.

Well, I never said I was neat . . .

I don't remember dropping the Coke bottle, but if it's there, I must have. Unless some other version of me left it there—

That *is* possible. The more I bounce around time, the more versions of me there are; many of us seem to be overlapping, but I have observed Dans and Dons doing things that I never have or never will—at least I don't intend to—so if they exist in this timeline, they must be other versions, just "passing through."

Either they're around to react to me, or I'm supposed to react to them. Or both. Certain fluxes must keep occurring, I guess—I assume there are mathematical formulae for expressing them, but I'm no mathematician—which necessitate two or more versions of myself coming into contact: such as the Don who came back through time to warn me against winning three million dollars at the race track on May 20.

That one was a situation where three versions of me had to exist simultaneously in one world: Dan, Don, and ultra-Don (who was excising himself). Other situations have been more complex; the more complex I become, the more *me*'s there are in this world.

The whole process is evolutionary. Every time Daniel Eakins eliminates a timeline, he's removing a non-viable one and replacing it with one that suits him better. The world changes and develops, always working itself toward some unknown utopia of his own personal design.

My needs and desires keep changing, so does the world. (I must be about thirty now. I have no way of keeping track, but I look about that age.) I have lived in worlds dedicated to the pursuit of pleasure—sexual fantasies come true. I have lived in other worlds too, harsher ones, for the sense of adventure. World War II was my private party.

But always, whenever I create a specialized world, I make a point of doing it very, very carefully with one or two easily reversed changes.

I do not want to get too far from *home*—meaning my own timeline. I do not want to get lost among alternate worlds with no way to get back and no way to find out what changes I made to create that alternate world.

So I make my changes one at a time and double-check

each one before introducing another. If I decide I do not like a world, I will know exactly how to excise it. (I thought I had done right when I kidnapped the baby Hitler and left him twenty years away from his point of origin, but that had serious repercussions on the world of 1975, so I had to put the baby back. Instead I let Hitler be assassinated by his own generals in 1944. Much neater.)

For a while I was on an anti-assassination kick. I have had the unique pleasure of tapping Lee Harvey Oswald on the shoulder (Yes, I know there were people who had doubts about who did it—but *I was there;* I know it was Oswald) just before he would have pulled the trigger. Then I blew his head off. (John Wilkes Booth, James Earl Ray, and Sirhan Sirhan were similarly startled. In two cases, though, I had to go back and excise my removal of the assassins. I didn't like the resultant worlds. Some of our heroes serve us better dead than alive.)

Once I created a world where Jesus Christ never existed. He went out into the desert to fast and he never came back.

The twentieth century I returned to was—different.

Alien.

The languages were different, the clothing styles, the maps, everything. The cities were smaller; the buildings were shorter and the streets were narrower. There were fewer cars and they seemed ugly and inefficient.

I could have been on another planet. The culture was incomprehensible.

I went back and talked myself out of eliminating Jesus Christ.

Look. I confess no great love for organized religion. The idea of Christianity (with a capital C) leaves me cold. Jesus was only an ordinary human being, I know that for a fact, and everything that's been done in his name has been a sham. It's been other people using his name for their own ends.

But I don't dare excise that part of my world.

I might be able to make a good case for Christianity if I wanted. After all, the birth of the Christian idea and its resultant spread throughout the Western Hemisphere was a significant step upward in human consciousness—the placing of a cause, a higher goal, above the goals of oneself. In this case, the cause is the kingdom of heaven to be created on Earth.

But I also know that Christianity has held back any *further* advances in human consciousness for the past thousand years. And for the past century it's been in direct conflict with its illegitimate offspring, Communism (again with a capital C). Both ask the individual to sacrifice his self-interest to the higher goals of the organization. (Which is okay by me as long as it's voluntary; but as soon as either becomes too big—and takes on that damned capital C—they stop asking for cooperation and start demanding it.)

Any higher states of human enlightenment have been sacrificed between these two monoliths.

So why am I so determined to preserve the Church?

Because, more than any other force in history, it has created the culture of which I am a product. If I eliminate the Church, then I eliminate the only culture in which I am a native. I become, literally, a man without a country.

Presumably there are worlds that are better than this one, but if I create them, it must be carefully, because I have to *live* in them too. I will be a part of whatever world I create, so I cannot be haphazard with them.

Just as a time-traveling Daniel Eakins keeps evolving toward a more and more *inevitable* version of himself, then so does the world he creates. It's a pretty stable world, especially in the years between 1970 and 2020.

Every so often it needs a "dusting and cleaning" to keep it that way, but it's a pretty good world.

Just as I keep excising those of *me* which tend to extremes, so am I excising those worlds which do not suit me. I experiment, but always come back.

I guess I'm basically a very conservative person.

*　　*　　*

Once in a while I wonder about the origins of the time-belt. Where did it come from?

Who built it—and why?

I have a theory about it, but there's no way to check for sure. Just as I am unable to return to the timeline of my origin, so is the timebelt unable to return to its. All I can do is hypothesize . . .

But figure it this way: at some point in some timeline, somebody invents a time machine. Somebody. Anybody. Makes no difference, just as long as it gets invented.

Well, that's a pretty powerful weapon. The ultimate weapon. Sooner or later some power-hungry individual is going to realize that. Possession and use of the timebelt is a way for a man to realize his every dream. He can be king of the world. He can be king of *any* world—every world!

Naturally, as soon as he can, he's going to try to implement his ideas.

The first thing he'll do is excise the world in which the timebelt was invented, so no one else will have a belt and be able to come after him. Then he'll start playing around in time. He'll start rewriting his own life. He'll start creating new versions of himself; he'll start evolving himself across a variety of timelines.

Am I the trans-lineal beneficiary of that person?

Or maybe the timebelt began another way—

It looks like a manufactured product, but very rugged. Could it have been built for military uses? Could some no-longer existent nation have planned to rule throughout history by some vast timebelt-supported dictatorship? Am I the descendant of a fugitive who found a way to excise that tyranny?

Or—and this is the most insane of all—is it that somewhere there's a company that's manufacturing and selling timebelts like transistor radios? And anyone who wants one just goes to his nearby department store, plunks $23.95 down on the counter and gets all his dreams fulfilled?

Crazy, isn't it?

But possible.

As far as the home timeline is concerned, all those people using timebelts have simply disappeared. As far as each subjective traveler knows, he's rewriting all of time. It makes no difference either way; the number of alternate universes is infinite.

The more I think about it, the more likely that latter possibility seems.

Consider: it's the far future. You've almost got utopia— the only thing that keeps every man from realizing all of his dreams is the overpopulation of the planet Earth. So you start selling timebelts—you give them away—pretty soon every man is a king and the home world is depopulated to a comfortable level. The only responsibility *you* need worry about is policing yourself, not letting schizoid versions of yourself run around your timeline. (Oh, you could, I suppose, but could you sleep nights knowing there was a madman running loose who wanted to kill you?) The reason is obvious—you want to keep your own timelines stable, don't you?

Is that where it started?

Is that where Uncle Jim came from? Did he buy himself a timebelt and excise out the world that created it?

I don't know.

I suspect, though, that a timebelt never gets too far from the base timeline, and that the user-generated differences in the timelines are generally within predictable limits.

Because the instructions are in English.

Wherever it was manufactured, it was an English-speaking world. With all that implies. History. Morals. Culture. Religion. (Perhaps it was my home timeline where the belt began, perhaps just a few years in my future.)

Obviously the belt was intended for people who could read and understand its instructions. Otherwise, you could kill yourself. Or worse. You could send yourself on a one-way trip to eternity. (Read the special cautions.)

If the average user is like me, he's too lazy to learn a new language (especially one that might disappear forever with his very next jump), so anyone with a timebelt is likely to keep himself generally within the confines of his own culture. His changes will be minimal: he'll alter the results of a presidential election, but he won't change the country that holds that election. At least not *too* much. So the timebelts remain centered around the English-speaking nexus.

Those users who do go gallivanting off to Jesus-less universes will find themselves in worlds where English never developed. If they elect to stay, making it their new homeline, they can continue to spin off any number of themselves. But when the last version dies, that's where the belt stops. There's no one in that timeline who can read the directions.

A timebelt either stays close to home, or it stops being used. Should anyone attempt to use the belt, they'll probably eliminate themselves (you can't learn time-tracking by trial and error). It's crude, but effective. It's an automatic way of eliminating extreme variations of the homeline.

Just *what* the homeline is, though, I'll never know.

I've come so far in the ten or more years I've been using the belt that I'm not sure I even remember where *I* started.

I wish I could talk to Uncle Jim about it, but I can't. He's not in this timeline.

Too late I went looking for him, but he wasn't there. I don't know what it was, I've made so many changes, but something I did must have excised him. I don't know what to undo to find him.

I've removed myself from my last real contact with—with what? Reality?

I've never been so lonely in my life.

*   *   *

Maybe I'm lost in time.

It's a fact, I don't know where I am.

I went looking for Uncle Jim and couldn't find him. When I realized that I must have accidentally excised him (probably by one of my "revisions" in this world), I went looking for myself. If I caught myself on May 19, 1975, when I was given the timebelt, perhaps I could keep myself from editing out my uncle.

But I wasn't there either.

I do not exist in this timeline.

There is no Daniel Eakins here, nor any evidence to indicate that he ever existed.

In this world I have no more past than I did in the Jesus-less world. I have no origins.

And no future either.

If I cannot find younger versions of myself, perhaps there are older versions—but if there are, where are they? I have met no one in this timeline, at least no one who I have not become within a few days.

Where is my future?

The house has never seemed so empty.

The poker game is deserted, the pool table is empty, the bedroom lies unused. The stereo is silent, the swimming pool is still, and I feel like a ghost walking through a dead city. The crowds of me have vanished.

My past has been excised, and I have no future.

Am I soon to die in this timeline?

Or do I just desert it?

Is that why I'm no longer here?

(Am I hiding from myself—why doesn't a Don come back to help me?)

If this timeline is a dead end, then where am I going?

I wish I had my Uncle Jim.

I wish I had my Don.

Or even my Dan. Sweet Dan . . .

I've never been so scared.

Don, if you read this, please help me.

* * *

I must be logical about this.

One of two things has happened—is about to happen.

The *me* I am about to become has obviously found a new timeline. Either he doesn't want to come back to this one, or he is unable to. Perhaps he has made some change that he can't undo. Perhaps he doesn't even know what that change is.

Is it a change in the world timeline? Has he created a universe where Aristotle never existed? Or did he accidentally kill Pope Sixtus the Fifth? Maybe it was something subtle, like stepping on a spider . . . or fathering a child who shouldn't have been. Whatever it was, has the Daniel Eakins I am about to be lost himself in some strange and alien timeline?

I keep remembering the timeline where Jesus never lived—am I to be lost in a world like that?

Or is the change something else? Is it in me instead?

Am I about to make some drastic alteration in my personality? Something I can't excise? Something I won't want to excise?

Something I am *unable* to excise? What if I turn myself into a paraplegic? Or a mongoloid idiot, incapable of understanding?

Or—am I on the verge of killing myself? Or worse?

For the first time since I was given the timebelt, I am unable to see the future—my own personal future—and it scares me.

Now I know what those *other* people feel. The ones who aren't me.

* * *

Suppose—just suppose—that I wanted to meet another version of myself:

I travel through time and there I am, an earlier or later Dan. I can stay as long as I want and without any obligation to relive the time from the other side. After all, we're really two different people. Really.

The first time I used the timebelt I met Don. Then I had thought that there was only one of me and that the seeming existence of two of us was just an illusion. Now I know that was wrong.

There's an infinite number of me, and the existence of one is an illusion.

An illusion? Yes, but an illusion as real to the subjective point of view as the illusion of travel through time. It makes no difference to *me*.

As far as *I'm* concerned, *I'm* real.

I think I exist, therefore I exist. I think.

And so do all the others.

Now. How do I go about meeting one of them?

One of those *other* versions of myself, one of the *separate* versions?

Not one who is simply me at some other part of my subjective life—as so many of the Dons and Dans are—but a Daniel Eakins who has gone off in some entirely *different* direction. How would I meet him?

The problem is one of communication. How do I let him know that I want to meet him? How do I get a message across the timelines?

Well, let's see . . .

I could put something in the timebelt itself, a date and location perhaps, then substitute it into Uncle Jim's package . . .

No. That part of my past no longer exists in this world. I excised it—remember?

Well, then, how about if I left a message far in the past . . .

No, that wouldn't work. *Where* would I leave it? How would I—how would *he*—know where to look for it? How could I even be sure of its enduring for the several thousand years it would have to? (Besides, I'm not sure it

would exist in any of the timelines that branched off before I got myself into this dead end. Changes in the
timestream are supposed to be cumulative, not retro-
active.)

I guess the answer to my question about getting a message across the timelines is obvious: I don't. There simply
isn't any working method of trans-temporal communication. At least none that's foolproof.

But that doesn't mean I still can't meet another version
of myself.

I meet different versions of myself all the time. The
mild variants. The only reason I haven't run into a
distant variant is that we haven't been tramping a common ground.

If I want to find such a variant, I have to go somewhere he's likely to be.

Suppose that somewhere there's another me—a distant
me—who's thinking along the same lines: he wants to
meet a Daniel Eakins who is widely variant from himself.

What memories do we have in common?

Hmm, only those that existed before we were given
the timebelt . . .

That's it, of course!

Our birthday.

*   *   *

I was born at 2:17 in the morning, January 24, 1956, at the
Sherman Oaks Medical Center, Sherman Oaks, California.

Of course, in *this* timeline, I hadn't been born—
wouldn't be born. Something I had done had excised my

birth; but I knew the date I would have been born and so did every other Dan.

It was the logical place to look.

In 1977 the Sherman Oaks Medical Center was a row of seven three- and four-story buildings lining Van Nuys Boulevard just north of the Ventura Freeway.

In 1956 it comprised only two buildings, one of which was strictly doctors' offices.

I twinged a little bit as I drove down Van Nuys Boulevard of the mid-fifties. I'd been spending most of my time in the seventies. I hadn't realized . . .

The two movie theatres were still the Van Nuys and the Rivoli. Neither had been remodeled yet into the Fox or the Capri. Most of the tall office buildings were missing; there were too many tacky little stores lining the street.

And the cars—my god, did people actually drive those things? They were boxy, high, and bulky; their styling was atrocious—Fords and Chevys with the beginnings of tail fins and double headlights; Chryslers and Cadillacs with too much chrome and too much styling. And Studebakers—and DeSotos!

There was a big vacant field where I remembered a blue-glass slab-sided building that stretched for more than a block. But the teenage hangout across the street from it was still alive, still a hangout.

I twinged, because in 1977 I had left a city. This was only a small town, busy in its own peaceful way, but still a small town. Why had I remembered it as being *exciting?*

As I approached the Medical Center itself, I realized with a start that something was missing. Then it hit me—in 1956 the Ventura Freeway hadn't been built yet, didn't extend to Van Nuys Boulevard. (I wondered if the big red Pacific Electric Railroad cars were still running. I didn't know when they had finally stopped, but the tracks had remained for years.)

I'd seen Los Angeles in its earlier incarnations, but the Los Angeles of 1930 had always seemed like another city, like a giant Disneyland put up for Danny the perpetual tourist. It wasn't real. But this—this I *recognized*. I could see the glimmerings of my own world here, its embryonic beginnings, the bones around which the flesh of the future would grow.

I parked my '76 'Vette at the corner of Riverside Drive and Van Nuys, ignoring the stares of the curious. I'd forgotten what I was doing and brought it back with me. So what; let them think it was some kind of racer. I couldn't care less. I was lost in thought.

I'd been living my whole life around the same three years. Sure, I'd gone traveling off to other eras, but those had been just *trips*. I'd always returned to 1976 as home.

I'd folded and compressed my whole life into a span of just a few months.

Consequently, I lived in a world where the landscape never changed. *Never*.

They'd been building the new dorm for the college for as long as I could remember. They'd been grading for the new freeway forever. (Oh, I knew what the finished structures would look like. I'd even driven the new freeway; but the time that I knew as *home* was frozen. Static. Unchanging.)

I'd lived in the same year for over ten subjective years. I'd grown too used to the idea that *home* would endure forever. For me, the San Fernando Valley was a stable entity. I'd forgotten what a dynamically alive city it was because I'd lost the ability to see its growth—

—because I no longer traveled linearly through time.

104

Other people travel through time in a straight line. For them, growth is a constant process, perceived only when the changes are major ones, or when there is something to compare them against.

To me, growth is—

—it doesn't exist. Every time I jump, I *expect* the world to change. I never equate any era with any other.

Until now, that is.

I *knew* this city; I'd grown up here—but I'd forgotten that it existed. I'd forgotten what it was like to be a part of the moving timestream, to grow up with a city, to see it change as you change . . .

I'd forgotten so much.

So much.

* * *

There was no one at the hospital, of course.

That is, I wasn't there—there were no other versions of Daniel Jamieson Eakins waiting to meet me.

I should have known it, of course. My birthday fell within the range of changes I'd been making. I was the only *me* in this timeline. If I wanted to find another me, I'd have to go outside the scope of my temporal activity. I'd have to go into the past. *Deep* into the past.

The only way to escape the effects of any change is to jump back to a point before it happened.

I'd been making changes for the past two hundred years. If I was to meet a variant Dan, we'd both have to go back beyond that span.

But how far back?

I stood by the car, jingling my keys indecisively. The

one location I was sure of was this hospital; the one date, my birthday.

Okay—

This spot. The middle of the San Fernando Valley. The date: January 24. My birthday.

—one thousand years ago. Exactly.

I got in the car, set the timebelt to include it, and tapped twice—

* * *

POP!

I'd been expecting it, but the jump-shock was still severe. The pain of it is directly proportional to the amount of mass making the jump.

Rubbing myself ruefully, I opened the door and got out.

My Corvette and I were in the middle of a flat brown plain. Scraggly plants and bushes all around. I recognized the Hollywood Hills to the southeast. Crisp blue sky. Unreal; no smog. And dry, almost desertlike ground stretching emptily to the purple-brown mountains that surrounded the valley. The San Bernardino range had never looked so forbidding; those black walls at the far northeast end were the largest feature of the landscape. For once they were undimmed by human haze, undwarfed by human buildings, unscarred by human roads. I gazed in awe; I'd never really noticed them before.

"Well?" said a female voice behind me. "Are you going to stand there and admire the view all day?"

I whirled—

—she was beautiful.

Almost my height. Hair the same color brown as mine. Eyes the same color green, soft and down-turned. The same cast of features, only slightly more delicate. She could have been my sister.

She indicated the car with a nod and a giggle. "Are you planning to drive somewhere?"

"I—uh, no—that is—I didn't know what I was planning. I— Hey, *who are you?*"

"Diane."

"Diane? Is that all?"

She twinkled. "Diana Jane Eakins. Hey, what's the matter? Did I say something wrong?"

"I'm Dan!" I blurted. "Daniel Eakins. Daniel Jamieson Eakins—"

"Oh—" she said. And then it sunk in. *"Oh!"*

* * *

The silence was embarrassing.

"Uh . . ." I said. "I have this timebelt."

"So do I. My Aunt Jane gave it to me."

"I got mine from my Uncle Jim."

She pointed to a gazebo-like affair about a hundred yards off. "Would you like to sit down?"

"Did you bring that with you?"

"Uh-huh. Do you like it?"

I followed her through the weeds. "Well, it's . . . different." Judging from its distance and the angle from the car, she had put it up in the hospital parking lot.

"It's more comfortable than a sports car," she said.

I shrugged. "I won't deny it." I recognized the gazebo as a variation of the Komfy-Kamper (1998): *"All the comforts of home in a single unit.*" I wondered if I should reach out for her hand. She was looking strangely at me too. I reached out . . .

We walked side by side the short remaining distance. "Why did you come back here?" I asked.

"To see if anyone else would," she said. "I was lonely."

"Me too," I admitted. "I suddenly discovered I couldn't find myself. I'd excised my past and there didn't seem to be any me in the future—"

"You too? That's what happened to me. I couldn't even find my Aunt Jane."

"—so I thought I'd come looking for a variant Dan and find out what happened."

I stopped abruptly. I certainly had found a variant Dan. About as variant as I could get . . . I wondered what I was shaped like under those clothes.

She let go of my hand and took a step back; she cocked her head curiously. "Why are you looking at me like that?"

"You're very pretty."

She flushed, then she recovered. "You're kind of cute too." She peered closely at me. "I've always wondered what I would look like as a boy. Now I know; I'd be very handsome." Impulsively she put her hands on my chest. "And very nicely built too—not too much muscle, not so many as to look brutish; just enough to look manly."

Now it was my turn to be embarrassed. I dropped my gaze to her breasts.

"You can touch them if you want."

I wanted to. I did.

They were nice, not flabby. Firm.

"I don't wear a bra," she said.

"I noticed."

"Do I pass inspection?" she whispered.

"Oh, yes," I said. "Very much so."

She pressed close to me, she moved her face up to mine . . .

The kiss lasted for a very long, long time.

*　*　*

The sun was lowering behind the western hills; the sky was all shades of purple and orange. Twilight was a gray-blue haze.

We'd been talking for hours. We'd stopped to eat and then we'd talked some more.

We had pulled the shades on three sides of the gazebo and turned the heat up. We sat naked in the glow of the electric fire and watched the sunset.

"The more I look at you, the prettier you get," she murmured.

"You too." I stretched across the heater and kissed her.

"Careful," she said after a moment. "Don't burn anything off. We may want to use it again."

"I hope so." I kissed her again, while she cupped me protectively. I moved closer.

We lay there side by side for a while. "I can't get over how good you feel." Her hands stroked up and down my back, my sides, my legs; my hands held her shoulders, her breasts; I kissed them gently, I kissed her eyelids too.

She looked up at me. "I liked having you inside me. It was very good."

"I liked being inside you."

She hugged me tight. "I could stay like this forever."

"Me too."

There was silence. The night gathered softly. Our words hung in the air.

Finally I said, "You know, we could. We could stay here forever."

"Do you want to . . . ?"

"Yes," I whispered. I began to move again. "Oh, yes."

"Oh, Dan," she gasped. "Oh, my darling, my sweet, sweet Dan—"

"Oh, baby, yes—" I rearranged my position on top of her and again the silvery warmth tingled—

Exploded.

Delighted.

* * *

—slid into me.

He was around me and inside me, his arms and legs and penis; we rocked and moved together, we fitted like one person. He filled me till I overflowed, kindled and enflamed—

We gasped and giggled and sighed and soared and sang and laughed and cried and leaped and flew and—

—dazzled and burst, exploding fireworks, surging fire—

We rustled and sighed. And died. And hugged and held on.

He was still within me. Sweet squeeze, warmth. I held him tight. I loved the feel of him, the taste of him. I loved the smell of him—the sweaty sense of masculine man. Musky. I melted, under him, around him.

Loved him.

* * *

January night. Cold wind. We pulled the last shade.

There was just one more thing. I had to make it complete.

"Dan," I whispered. "I have to tell you something."

"What?" In the pink light, his face was glowing.

I took a breath. "I—I'm not a virgin."

"Of course not," he grinned. "We just took care of that."

"No, that's not what I meant. I wasn't a virgin—before."

"Oh?" His voice went suddenly strange.

"I mean—" I forced myself to go on. I had to tell him everything or it wouldn't be any good. "I was only a 'technical virgin.' I'd never done it with a boy before. You were the first."

"Oh," he said quietly. "Then that means you did it with . . . girls?"

"Only Donna—and Diana. I mean, I only did it with myself. When I was Donna, I—"

He cut me off gently, "I know."

"Is it all right?" I had to know. "You're not disappointed in me?"

"Of course not. I—understand."

"I only did it because I was lonely."

"No," he said slowly, shaking his head. "You wanted to do it and you enjoyed it. You did it because you're the only person you can trust, the only person you feel completely at ease with, and you wanted to express your feelings and your affection. You did it because you loved yourself."

"I—yes, you're right." I couldn't deny it. I fidgeted with my hands; I was afraid to look at him.

"Diana," he whispered. "Think a minute. About me. I'm both Don and Dan. I'm the male reflection of you."

His eyes were bright.

"Did you—?" I couldn't finish the question.

But he knew what I meant. He nodded. "We did—I did."

I thought about that. Dan. Diane.

Dan. Diane.

Boy. Girl.

Same. Person.

And suddenly I was crying. Crying, sobbing into his arms. "Oh, Dan, I'm so sorry—"

He stroked my hair. "There, there, baby, there's nothing to be sorry about, nothing at all."

"I'm so stupid—"

"No, you're not. You were smart enough to come looking for me, weren't you?"

"Oh, no—I didn't know what I was looking for. I just didn't want to be alone any more."

"Neither did I. I didn't know what I wanted either, but you're just perfect—"

"So are you—" I wiped at the tears on his chest. Then started crying again. "Oh, hold me, Dan, hold me—be a man to me, be a man. Be what Donna never was, never could be. Fill me with your love. I want you inside me again."

"Oh, yes, baby. Yes, yes. Yes— Oh, Danny, I love you."

"Donna, I love you too!"

* * *

The sensuousness of sex. The maleness of me. The femaleness of her. The physical sensations of strength and warmth. Flesh against smooth flesh. Firm resistance, supple yielding.

Sex with Diane is different from any kind of sex I have

112

ever had before. There is something boyish about her that I find strangely attractive, yet deliciously feminine. (I put my arms around her and she is neither male nor female, but a little of each. And there is something feminine in me that she responds to. Perhaps it is a quality that is common to both of us and independent of physical gender. An androgynous quality. My body may be male or it may be female, but I am neither—I am me.)

I keep thinking of Danny, and it is hard not to make comparisons between the two of them, even though I know it is unfair to both. But Danny and I (Don and I) have been through so much together, have meant so much to each other . . .

Diane lacks Danny's intensity (yes), but Danny could never match her sensuality. The sheer *physical* delight of her body, the perfect matching of male to female, the tenderness of her response; all of these combine to make sex with her an experience that is new to me. I delight in being with her, in being inside of her, just as she delights in opening to me. That yearning slit . . .

I see her as something special. Not a new person, no, but another reflection of myself. Another Danny perhaps— and in the most different guise of all.

Yes. Danny with a vagina.

Think of her as *he*. It is the quality of Danny-ness I see in him that is so intriguing, so independent of sexuality. There is a Danny trapped inside that female body screaming to let me in. Just as there is a Diane inside me.

I cannot help but like it.

We enjoy our physical roles as we have never enjoyed them before; at least I know *I* do; but deep inside is a sense of—loss. I think I *loved* my Danny more. And I think I know why.

With Danny, the physical forms were identical; the

mental roles could be arbitrary. It was just me and him. I didn't have to be male, I didn't have to be dominant. With Don I could be weak, with Don I could cry.

With Diane, I am limited to one role only; the physical determines it; I must be a man to her woman. (Danny is a woman. Danny has limited our roles.) There is no other relationship for either of us.

The relationship is not unenjoyable. Indeed, it is the most joyous of all. But still, there is that sense of loss . . .

* * *

We have been together how long?

Months, it must be.

We have a home on the edge of prehistory, a villa on the shores of what someday will be called Mission Bay. It's a sprawling mansion on a deserted coast, a self-contained unit; it has to be, because we brought it back to the year 2000 B.C. A honeymoon cottage for the outcasts of time.

The sea washes blue across yellow sands. Sea gulls wheel and dive, cawing raucously. The sun is bright in an azure sky. And the only footprints are ours.

We live a strange kind of life in our timeless world.

Loneliness is unknown to us; yet neither of us ever lacks for privacy. We see each other only when *both* of us want it. Never can one force himself on the other. That's part of being a time traveler.

I cannot journey to her future, nor can she to mine. When we bounce forward, I am in Danny's world, she is in Diane's. The only place we can meet is in the past, because only the past is unaffected by both of us.

114

Should either of us need to be alone, we simply bounce to a different point in time. (I have seen the ruins of this mansion standing forlorn and alone, swept by the sands and washed by the sea, while the sun lies orange in the west. These walls will be dust by the time of Christ.)

Returning, I am in her arms again. I am there because I want to be there.

She vanishes too, but only momentarily; she returns in a different dress and hair style. I know she has been gone longer than I have seen, but I know she comes back to me with her desire at its fullest. I open my arms.

We have never had an argument. It is impossible when either of you can disappear at the instant of displeasure. All of our moments are happy ones. Life with Diane is almost idyllic.

Almost.

Today she told me she was pregnant.

And I'm not sure how I feel about that. There is a sense of joy and wonder in me—but I am also disturbed. Jealous that something else, some*one* else, can make her glow with such happiness. The look on her face as she told me—I have seen that intensity only in her climax.

I know I shouldn't be, but I am bothered that I cannot give her such prolonged intensity of joy. And I am bothered that someone else is inside her. Someone other than me.

And yet, I'm happy. Happy for her, happy for me. I don't know why, but I know that this baby must be something special.

It *must* be.

❊   ❊   ❊

The baby proves something that I have suspected for a long time. My life is out of control. I am no longer the master of my own destiny.

There is little that I can do with this situation. Except run from it.

Or can I . . . ?

* * *

Being pregnant is a special kind of time.

Within me there is life, helpless and small; I can feel it move. I can feel it grow. I wait eagerly for the day of its entrance into this world so I can hold it and touch it. Love it and feed it, hold it to my breasts.

This is a special baby. It will be. I know it will be. I am filled with wonder. I see my body in the mirror, swollen and beautiful. I run my hands across my bulging stomach in awed delight. This is something Donna could never have given me. (I miss her though; I wish she were here to share this moment. She is, of course. She *will* be here when I need her.)

Oh, there is discomfort too, more than I had expected— the difficulties in bending over and walking, the back pains and the troubles in the bathroom, the loginess and the nausea—but it's worth it. When I think of the small beautiful wonder which will soon burst into my life, the whole world turns pink and giggly.

I feel that I'm on the threshold of something *big*.

* * *

The baby was born this morning.

It was a boy. A beautiful, handsome, healthy boy.

I am delighted. And disappointed. I had wanted a girl. A girl . . .

* * *

In 1993 the first genetic-control drug was put on the market. It allowed a man and woman to choose the sex of their unborn child.

In 2035 in-utero genetic tailoring became practical. The technique allowed a woman to determine which of several available chromosomes in the egg and sperm cells would function as dominants; the only provision was that the tailoring must be done within the first month of pregnancy.

In 2110 extra-utero genetic tailoring was widespread. The process allowed the parent to program the shape of his offspring. A computer-coded germ plasm could be built, link by amino-acid link, implanted into a genetically neutral egg, then carefully cultured and developed, eventually to be implanted in a womb, real or artificial.

I do not want to design a whole child. I just want a baby girl. I want her identical to me. I will have to go back and see Diane before she gets pregnant, but that should be the easy part.

I will not tell Dan this; I think this is a decision that I have to make myself. The baby is mine and so is the decision. My son will be a girl.

* * *

The baby was born this morning.

It was a girl. A beautiful, pink little girl.

I am delighted. And disappointed. I had wanted a boy. A boy . . .

* * *

I will not tell Diane this; this is a decision that I have to make myself. (And there are ways that it can be done so that she will never know. I know when the child was conceived and I know which drugs to take beforehand. I will have to either replace Danny, or make him take the injection, but she will never suspect.)

My daughter will be a son.

* * *

Why do I keep coming back?

I get on her nerves, she gets on mine. We argue about the little things; we make a point of fighting with each other. Why?

Last night we were lying in bed, side by side, just lying there, not doing anything, just listening to each other breathe and staring at the ceiling. She said, "Danny?"

I said, "Yes?"

She said, "It's over, isn't it?"

I nodded. "Yes."

She turned to me then and slid her arms around me. Her cheeks were wet too.

I held her tight. "I'm sorry," I said. "I wanted it to work so much."

118

She sniffed. "Me too."

We held onto each other for a long time. After a while I shifted my position, then she shifted hers. She rolled over onto her back and I slid on top of her. She was so slender, so intense. Her hand stroked me gently, then guided me in. We moved together in silence, only the sound of our breathing. We remembered and pretended, each of us lost in our own thoughts, and wishing it hadn't come to this.

The sheets were cool in the night and she was warm and silky. If only it could be like this all the time . . .

But it couldn't. It was over. We both knew it.

           *   *   *

I'm not going back any more.

Whatever there was between us is gone. We both know it. The bad moments outweigh the good. There is no joy left.

Besides, she isn't there all the time anyway.

I have brought my son forward with me; I will find him a home in the twentieth century. And I will watch over him. I will be very careful not to accidentally excise him. He is all I have left.

It's not without regret that I do this. I miss my Diane terribly. But something happened to us; the magic disappeared, the joy faded, and the delight we had found in each other ceased to exist.

The last night . . . we made love mechanically, each seeking only our own physical satisfaction. Somehow, my feelings had become more important to me than hers. I wonder why?

Was it because I knew that I would never—*could never* —experience it from her side?

Perhaps . . .

Love with Diane was . . . sad. I could see the *me* in her, but I could never be that *me*.

And that meant that she wasn't really me. Not *really*. She was—somebody else.

I couldn't communicate with her. We used the same words, but our meanings were different. (They *must have* been different. She wasn't *me*.)

I'm sorry, Diane. I wanted it to work. I did. But I couldn't reach you. I couldn't reach you at all.

So.

I'll go back to my Danny. He'll understand. He's been waiting patiently for so long . . .

* * *

Oh God, I feel alone.

* * *

It's been years since I last added anything to this journal. I wonder how old I am now; I really have no way of telling.

Forty? Fifty? Sixty? I'm not sure. The neo-procaine treatments I've been taking in 1991 seem to retard all physical evidence of aging. I could still be in my late thirties. But I doubt it. I've done so much. Seen so much.

I've been living linearly—semi-linearly. Instead of bouncing haphazardly around time, I've set up a home in 1956, and as it travels forward through time at its stately day-to-day pace, I am traveling with it.

Oh, I'm still using the future and the past, but not as before.

Before, I was young, foolish. I was like a barbarian at the banquet. I gulped and guzzled; I ate without tasting. I rushed through each experience like a tourist trying to see twenty-one European cities in two weeks and enjoying none of them.

Now I'm a gourmet. I savor each day. I taste the robustness of life, but not so hurriedly as to lose its delicate overtones. I've given up the hectic seventies for the quiet fifties—the fifties are as early as I dare go without sacrificing the cultural comforts I desire. They are truly a magic moment in time, a teeterboard suspended between the wistful past and the soaring future.

The fifties are a great time to live. They are close enough to the nation's adventurous past to still bear the same strident idealism, yet they also bear the shape of the developing future and the promise of the technological wonders to come. Transistor radios are still marvelous devices and color television is a delicious miracle, but blue skies are commonplace and the wind blows with a freshness from the north that hints at something wild—and suggests that the city is only a temporary illusion, a mirage glowing against a western desert.

Brave highways crisscross the state—and strangely, with a minimum of billboards, it seems. The roads are still new; they are the foundation for the great freeways of the future. This is the threshold of that era, but it is still too soon for them to be overburdened with traffic and ugliness. Driving is still an adventure.

The hills around Los Angeles are still uncut and green with the city's own special color of vegetation. Dark trees and dry grass. A cool kind of day. The fifties are a peaceful time, a quiet sleeping time between two noisy bursts of years, a blue and white time filled with sweet yellow days, music and bright-smelling memories . . .

Actually, it's 1961 as I write this. The fifties have ended and their magic is fading quickly. A young President has stamped a new dream on the nation and the frenetic stamp and click of the seventies can already be heard. The years are impatient; they tumble over each other like children, each rushing eagerly for its turn—and each in turn tumbling inexorably into the black whirlpool of forevertime lost. Well, not lost, not to me.

I have watched the fading of the fifties three times now, and perhaps I shall return again for a fourth. Perhaps . . .

*   *   *

Last week, in a mood of wistfulness for times lost, I went jaunting again. I went back to the past, to the house where Diane and I lived for such a short, short, long time.

One of the walls had collapsed and the wind blew through the rooms. A fine layer of clean, dry dust covered everything. The pillars and drapes stood alone on the cold plain.

My own doing, of course. I had not come back far enough, but I was afraid if I journeyed too far back, I would see *her* again.

And yet—I do want to see her again.

Just a little bit farther back . . .

*   *   *

And this time the house was not ruined. Just abandoned. Empty and waiting. My footsteps knocked hollowly across the marble floors.

Was she here? Had she been here at all?

There was no way of knowing.

I found my way to her rooms. Despite the acrid sunlight, her chambers were cold. I opened closets at random, pulled out drawers. Many of her silks were still here. Forgotten? Or just discarded?

A shimmering dress, ice-cream pastel and deep forest-green—I pressed my nose into the sleek shining material, seeking a long-remembered smell, a sweet-lemony fragrance with an undertone of musk. The clean smell of a woman . . .

Her smell is there, but faint. I dropped the dress. I am touched with incredible sadness.

And then a sound, a *step*—

I ran for the other room, calling.

But there was no one there.

Perhaps, perhaps, just a little bit farther back.

The day *after* the last day I was there. So many years ago . . .

✦ ✦ ✦

The air conditioner hums. The house is alive again.

And my Diane is beautiful, even prettier than I remembered. Her auburn hair shimmers in the sunlight. She moves with the grace of a goddess, and she wears even less, a filmy thing of lace and silk. I can see the sweet pinkness of her skin.

She hasn't seen me yet. I am here in the shadows, deep within the house. It has been too long. It hurts too much to watch.

Abruptly, puzzlement clouds her face. She comes rushing in from the patio. "Danny? Is that you?" Eagerness. "Are you back?"

And then she saw me.

"Danny? What's happened? Are you all right? You look" —and then she realized—"*old.*"

"Diane," I blurted. "I came back because I loved you too much to stay away any more."

She was too startled to answer. She dropped her eyes and whispered, "I loved you too, Danny." Then she looked at me again. "But you're not Danny any more. You're someone else."

"But I am Danny—" I insisted.

She shook her head. "You're not the same one."

I took a step forward, I reached as if to embrace her. She took a quick step back. "No, please, don't."

"Diane, what's the matter?"

"Danny—" There were tears running down her cheeks. "Danny, why did you stay away so long? Look what you've done to yourself. You've gotten *old.* You're not my Danny any more. You're—you're not young." She sniffled and wiped quickly. "I came back, Dan. I couldn't stay away either. I came back to wait for you and hope that you'd come back too. But look at you. You waited too long to come back."

"Diane, you loved me once. I'm still *me.* I'm still Danny. I have the same memories. Remember how you cried in my arms the last night we were together? Remember how we used to fix dinner together in the kitchen? Remember the—"

"Stop. Oh, stop. Please—" And suddenly she was in my

124

arms. Crying. "I loved you so much. So much. But you went away. How could you—how could you stay away so long? I thought you loved me too."

"Oh, baby, yes. I did. I *do*. I love you too much. That's why I came back—" I held her tightly to me, she was so warm.

"But why not sooner? Why did you stay so long?"

"Oh, let's not think about that. I'm back, that's all that counts." My hands could feel the tender silkiness of her skin. I remembered how I used to caress her and I slid into the motions almost automatically. Her breasts were soft, yet firm. Her hips were firm, yet soft. Her skin was so sheer—

"What are you doing?" She made as if to pull away.

"Oh, baby, baby, please—"

"Oh, no—not now, I couldn't. Please don't make me."

"Diane, I still love you—" The youthfulness of her body . . .

"Oh, no. It's only words. Words. You're saying them as if they're a magic charm to get me into bed." She backed away, wiping at her eyes. "I'm sorry, Danny, I really did love you, but I can't any more. You've"—she hesitated here—"changed. Mentally too. You don't care about *me* any more, do you?" She grabbed a robe and pulled it about her. "No, don't come any closer. Just listen a moment. There's a poem. It goes, 'Grow old along with me, the best is yet to be, the last of life for which the first was made . . .' I had thought—hoped—that was how it would be for us." Her voice caught. "But you've ruined it. It only took you a day to destroy both of our lives."

"No." I shook my head. "It didn't take a day. It took years. Diane, I'm sorry! Couldn't we . . . ?"

But she was gone. She had fled into the bedroom.

"Diane—"

And then the gentle *pop!* of air rushing in to fill an empty space told me how completely she was gone. How far she had fled.

* * *

Oh God. What have I done?

* * *

I could try again. All I need do is go back just a little earlier. I wouldn't make the same mistake this time.

I want my Diane. I must have my Diane.

I will have my Diane.

* * *

He's tried to talk me out of it, but I'm not going to let him stop me.

I know why he wants to keep me from going back. He's jealous of her. Because she'll have me and he won't.

But his way is wrong. I know that now. A man should have a woman. A real man needs a real woman.

Diane, sweet Diane. Please don't reject me again. I'm not old. I'm not. And you're so young . . .

* * *

Oh God, why?
Am I really that old and ugly?
No. I can't be. I can't be.
Do I dare go back and try again?

*   *   *

And again he tries to talk me out of it.
Damn him anyway!

*   *   *

Somewhere there is a Dan who is getting older and older. And he's working his way back through time, chasing Diane.

And each time Diane is that much younger and he's that much older. The gulf between them widens. Widens.

Oh, my poor, poor Dan. But he won't listen. He just won't listen.

I'm afraid to think of where he is heading. He'll work his way back through all the days of Diane, and every day she'll reject him. And Dan, poor Dan, he'll experience them all. Each time she rejects him will be the last day she'll spend in the fading past. So every day he'll go back one more day, and every day he'll be too old for her—

Until he gets back to the very first day. And then she'll be gone. There won't be any Diane at all. Just a memory.

And, in the end, he'll be there waiting for her—even before the first Danny. Waiting patiently for her first appearance, trying to re-create his lost love. But she won't show up. No, she'll have warned herself. Don't go back in time looking for a variant Diane. A grizzled old ghoul waits for you. No, she'll never come back at all.

Poor Dan. Poor, poor Dan.

*   *   *

And yet, the one I feel sorriest for is *young* Dan. He'll never know what he's missing.

Because, when he gets there, there won't be anyone there at all.

He'll never have a Diane. Ever. Old Dan will have chased them all away.

*   *   *

I wish I could change it all. I wish I could.

But I can't.

Dammit.

Now I know what it's like to have an indelible past—one that won't be erased and changed at will. It's frustrating. It's maddening. And it makes me wish I had been more careful and thoughtful.

But when you can erase your mistakes in a minute, you tend to get careless.

Until you make one you can't erase.

I feel uneasy because I think I didn't try hard enough, and yet, I can't think of anything I didn't do. I tried everything I could do to stop old Danny.

But it wasn't enough, and now I'm left with the results of what he's done.

We're *all* left with those results.

I could find young Danny in a minute, and I could warn him to go back to Diane right away, before it's too late, before he gets too old; but it wouldn't do any good. All he would find would be old Danny, sitting and waiting. Sitting and waiting.

Diane is gone. Forever. There's no way we can reach her. Old Danny has seen to that.

And there's no other place to look for her.

Any time. Any place. Any when that Diane might have thought to visit, there's an old Danny. Sitting and waiting.

I'll never see my Diane again.

(Can I content myself with Danny? My Danny? I'll have to.)

* * *

And yet, I wonder . . .

Perhaps somewhere there is an older Diane, one who has aged like me . . .

I wonder how I might find her.

* * *

Ah, but that way lies old Danny and madness.

It's not the answer.

* * *

There is a party at my house, the big place in 1999. A hundred and fifty-three acres of forest, lake, and meadow. I don't know how many *me*'s there are. The number varies.

The party is spread out across the whole summer. Several days in April and May, quite a few in June and July, and also some in August. I think there may be some in September too. Generally it starts about ten in the morning and lasts until I don't know when. It seems as if there's always a constant number of *Dan*s and *Don*s arriving and leaving.

It's like Grand Central Terminal, with passengers arriving and departing all the time, to and from destinations all over the world. Only, all the passengers are me and all the destinations are the same place, only years removed.

The younger Dans show up in May and June. They like the swimming and water-skiing and motorcycling. They like the hiking and climbing and open-air barbecues. They like the company of each other.

I prefer July. Most of the younger versions have faded by then. They're too nervous for me and they remind me too much of—Diane. They're too active, I can't keep up with them, and sometimes I think they're talking on a different plane. I prefer the men of July; they're more my age, they're more comfortable, and they're more moderate. We still do a lot of swimming and riding; I remember, I used to enjoy that very much; but most of the time we just like to take it easy.

I don't like the men of August. I've been there a few times, and they're too sedentary. No, they're too *old*. They just sit around and drink. And talk. And drink some more. Some of them look positively *wasted*.

Actually, it's the men of late August I really don't like.

The men of early August aren't that bad. It's just the old ones that bother me. Some of them are—filthy. Their minds, their mouths, their bodies. They want to touch me too much. And they call me their Danny, their little boy. (Several of them even seem senile.)

The men of early August are all right. They make me a little uncomfortable, but lately I've been visiting them more and more. Partly because it seems as if the younger men are taking over July and partly because *I'm* in August enough now to compensate for the older ones.

Several of them are very nice though. Very understanding. We've had some interesting talks. (And that surprises me too—that there are still things I can talk about with myself. I had thought I would have exhausted all subjects of conversation long ago. Apparently not.)

In the evenings we go indoors (there's a pool inside too) and listen to music (I have several different listening rooms) or play poker, or pool, or chess.

When I get tired (and when I want to sleep alone), there's a chart on the wall indicating which days and which beds are still unused. (The chart covers a span of several years. Well, I have to sleep somewhere . . .) I make a mark in any space still blank and that closes that date. Then I bounce to that point of time. (Generally I try and use those days in serial order. I have servants in the house then and it wouldn't do to confuse them.)

I'm still doing most of my living in the fifties, but when I'm in the mood for a party—and that's been more and more lately—I know where to find one. The poker games, for instance, are marathons. Or maybe it's only one poker game that's been going on since the party started. Whenever I get tired and want to quit, there's always a later me waiting for the seat.

But my endurance isn't what it used to be. I get tired

too fast these days. That's why I find the men of August so restful.

* * *

On August 13 a very strange thing happens. Has happened. Will happen.

I'd known about it for some time—that is, I'd known that something happens, because I don't attend the party linearly. I stay in a range of a week or two and bounce around within it; there's more variety that way.

After August 13 the mood of the party is changed. Subdued. Almost morbid. Most of me seem to know why, but they don't refer to it very often.

The last time something like this happened was just before I met Diane—when all the other versions of me had disappeared. I knew something was about to happen, but I didn't know what until I got there.

I have that same kind of feeling now. Too many of the older *me*'s are acting strange. Very strange. The more I hang around them, the more I see it.

I'm going to have to investigate August 13.

* * *

Is this it?

Three or four of the youngest Dannys are here; they're in a quieter mood than usual though, almost grim.

A couple of us frowned at them—they really weren't welcome here; they should have stayed in their own part of the party—but most of the rest of us tried at least to

132

tolerate them, hoping that they would lose interest soon and go back to their own time. "They're here to gape at us," complained one of me.

"Well, some of us are gaping right back," snapped another.

"God," whispered a third. "Was I ever really *that* young?"

And then there was a *pop!* as another me appeared. It was a common enough sound. Somebody was always appearing or disappearing at any given moment. But this one was different. A hush fell over the room. I turned and saw two of me reaching to support a third who had suddenly appeared between them. He was pale and gray; he was half slumped and holding his heart.

Apparently the jump-shock had been too much for him; that sudden burst of temporal energy jolts you every time you bounce through time. They helped him to a chair. Somebody was already there with a glass of water, somebody who had been through this before, I guess. And the younger Dans were murmuring among themselves; was this what they had come to see?

"Are you all right, old fellow?" someone asked the newcomer.

He grunted. He was old. He was very old. His hands were thin and weak. His forearms were parchment-covered bones, so were his legs. The skin of his face hung in folds and he was mottled with liver spots.

"Aaah," he gasped. "What day is it?"

"August 13."

"Thirteenth?" Slowly he pulled his features into a grimace. "Then I'm too soon. It's the twenty-third I want. I must have made the wrong setting."

"Take it easy. Just relax."

The oldster did so; it wasn't a matter of recognizing the wisdom of their words, he simply knew that he didn't have to hurry. A timebelt is a very forgiving device. Besides, he was too exhausted to move.

"What were you looking for?" asked one of the younger Dans. (They weren't me. I didn't remember ever having done this before, so they must have been variations from another timeline.)

The fragile gray man peered at them, abruptly frowning. "No," he croaked. "Too young. Too young. Got to talk to someone older. Those are just—just children."

Some of us shouldered the younger ones aside then. "What is it?" they asked. (Others hung back; had they heard it before? The room seemed emptier now. There were less than ten of me remaining. Several of us must have left.)

"Too tired," he gasped. "Came to warn you, but I'm too tired to talk. Let me rest . . ."

"Hey, have a heart, you guys. Don't press him." That was one of the quieter ones of us; I recognized him by his business suit, he had been hanging back and just watching most of the evening. "Take him in the bedroom and let him lie down for a while." He shoved through and picked up the frail old man—God, was he that light?—and carried him off to the downstairs bedroom. "You can talk to him later," he promised.

Out of curiosity, I followed. I helped him put the old man to bed, then he led me out. "You know what's going on, don't you?" I asked him.

He didn't answer, just got himself a chair and a book, and stationed himself in front of the door. "It might be too soon for you to worry about this," he said to me. "Why don't you go back to your party?" He opened the book and proceeded to ignore me.

There was nothing else to do, so I shrugged and went back into the other room. A little later a couple of other *me*'s tried to see how the old man was doing, but the business-suit-me wouldn't let them. He sat outside that room all night.

The party was considerably dampened by this incident. Most of the Dans faded away and the house became strangely deserted. Here and there, one or two of me were picking up dirty glasses and empty potato-chip dishes, but they only served to heighten the emptiness. They were like caretakers in a mausoleum.

I bounced forward to the morning, but the bedroom was empty and the business suit was gone too. So I bounced back an hour. Then another. This time he was there, still outside the door, still reading. When I appeared, he glanced up without interest. "Hmm? Is it that late already?" He opened his belt to check the time.

I started to ask him something, but he cut me off. "Wait a minute." He was resetting his belt. Before I could stop him he had tapped it twice and vanished.

I opened the bedroom door; the old man had vanished too.

My curiosity was too much. I bounced back fifteen minutes. Then fifteen minutes more. He was sleeping on the bed; his breath rasped slowly in and out.

I felt no guilt as I woke him; he'd had more than six hours undisturbed. I wanted to know what was so important. He came awake suddenly. "Where am I?" he demanded.

"August fourteenth," I told him.

That seemed to satisfy him, but he frowned at me in suspicion. "What do you want? Why'd you wake me?"

"What was supposed to happen last night?"

"Last night?"

"The thirteenth. You came to warn us of something . . ." I prompted.

"The thirteenth? That was a mistake. I wanted the twenty-third."

"Why? What happens on the twenty-third?"

He peered at me again. "You're too young." He pushed himself off the bed and stood unsteadily. And tapped his belt and vanished.

Damn.

*　*　*

Naturally, I went straight to the twenty-third.

My old man was there, of course. A dozen times over. Wrinkled, gnarled, and white. Their hands hovered in the air, or scrabbled across their laps like spiders. They clawed, they plucked.

But not all of them were that old. There were one or two that even looked familiar.

"Don?" I asked one who was wearing a faded shirt. If I remembered correctly, he had gotten that ketchup stain on it just a few hours ago at the poker table of the thirteenth.

He looked at me, startled. "Dan? You shouldn't be here. You're still too young. I mean, let us take care of this for now. You go back to the party."

"Huh?" I tried to draw him aside. "Just tell me what's going on."

"I can't," he whispered. "It wouldn't be a good idea—"

Abruptly, a familiar business suit was standing before us. Was it the same one? Probably. "I'll take over," he said to Don.

"Thanks," Don said, and fled in relief.

I looked at the other. "What's going on here?"

He looked at the clock in his timebelt. "In a few more minutes you'll find out." He took me by the arm and led me across the room. "Stand here. I'll stay right by you the

136

whole time. Don't say anything. Don't do anything. Just watch, this time around."

I shut my mouth and watched.

The air in the room was heavy. The few conversations still going were whispered, and the supposedly silent hum of the air conditioner was deafening. Almost all of these wrinkled faces, pale faces, were deathly. The few tan ones stood out like spotlights. They were grim too.

The old men. Their eyes were like holes in lampshade faces, but nothing glowed within. Their expressions were bleary. Uniform. Frightened.

And there were so many of them. More and more; the room was filling up. This house, so often a happy place, was now a cloister house of the infirm. The laughter of youth had shaded into the garish cackling of senility. What had been a firm grip on life had degenerated into a plucking and desperate claw, scratching on the edge of terror.

Who were these men—why could I not accept what I was seeing? And what drove them together here?

How old am I? (And here is the fear—) I don't know. I don't know.

Am I one of the tan faces or the pale ones? Does my skin hang in pale folds, bleached by age? (I touch my cheek hesitantly.)

As the air *pops!* softly—

—and the body that crumples to the floor is me.

*   *   *

Of course.

It was the jump-shock that killed him. Will kill *me*.

He was old. The oldest of them all. (But not so old as

to be distinguishable from the rest. He could have been any of them.)

There was silence in the room. Then a soft shadowed sigh, almost a sound of relief, as too many ancient lungs released their burden of breaths held too long.

They'd been expecting this, waiting for it—*eagerly?*—the curiosity of the morbid draws them again and again until the room is crowded with fearful old men. Each praying that, somehow, this time it won't happen. And each terrified that it will.

And perhaps—perhaps each is most afraid that the next time he comes to this moment, he will not be a witness, but the guest of honor himself . . .

* * *

Two of the younger men (younger? They were older than I—or were they?) moved to the body. It was still warm, but cooling rapidly. One of them clicked the belt open; the last setting on it was for 5:30, March 16, 1975. (Meaningless, of course. He could have come from there, or it could have been a date held in storage. There was no way of knowing.)

They took charge efficiently, as if they had done this before. Many times before. (And in a way, they had.) They slung the body between them, tapped their belts, and vanished.

"What're they going to do with him?" I asked the Don in the business suit.

"Take him back to his own time, to a place where he can be buried."

"Where?"

He shook his head. "Uh-uh. When the time comes, you'll know. Right now it wouldn't be a good idea."

"But the funeral—"

"Listen to me." He gripped my arm firmly. "You cannot go to the funeral. *None of us can.*"

"But why?"

"There'll be others there," he said. "*Others.* A man should attend his own funeral only once. Do you understand?"

After I thought about it awhile, I guessed I did.

* * *

As for me . . .

I'm almost afraid to use the timebelt now.

* * *

But now I know who I am.

I guess I've known for some time. I'm not sure when I realized; it was a gradual dawning, not a sudden flash of *aha*. I just sort of slipped into it as if it had been waiting for me all my life. I'd been heading toward it without ever once stopping to consider how or why.

And even if I had, would it have changed anything? I don't think so.

At first I tried to ignore the events of August 23. I went back to the earlier days of the party, but burdened as I was with the knowledge of what lurked only a few weeks ahead, I could not recapture the mood. (And that was sensed by the others; I was shunned as being an irritable and temperamental old variant. Nor was I the only one; there were several of us. We put a damper on the party wherever we went.)

For a while I brooded by myself. For a while I was terribly scared. In fact, I still am.

I don't want to die. But I've seen my own dead body. I've seen myself in the act of dying. Death comes black and hard, rushing down on me from the future, with no possible chance of escape. I wake up cold and shuddering in the middle of the night, and were it not for the fact that I am always there to hold and comfort myself, I would go mad. (And I still may do so—)

Uncle Jim once told me that a man must learn to live with the fact of his own mortality. A man must accept the fact of death.

But does that mean he must welcome it?

I'd thought that the measure of the success of any life form was its ability to survive in its ecological niche. But I'd been wrong. That doesn't apply to individuals, not at all—only to species as a whole.

If you want to think in terms of individuals, you have to qualify that statement. The measure of the success of any *individual* animal is based on its ability to survive long enough to reproduce. *And* care for the young until they are able to care for themselves.

I have met half that requirement. I've reproduced.

(It's said that the only immortality a man can achieve is through his children. I understand that now.)

I went back to 1956 to bring up my son. He was right where I had left him.

I named him Daniel Jamieson Eakins, and I told him I was his uncle. His Uncle Jim.

Yes. That's who I am.

140

In many ways, Danny is a great joy to me. I am learning as much from him as he is learning from me. He is a
beautiful child and I relish every moment of his youth.
I relive it by watching it. Sometimes I stand above his
crib and just watch him sleep. I yearn to pick him up and
hug him and tell him how much I love him—but I let
him sleep. I must avoid smothering him. I must let him
be his own man.

And I yearn to leap ahead into the future and meet the
young man he will become. It will be me, of course, starting all over again. Wondrously, I have come full circle.
Once more I am in a timeline where I exist from birth to
death. So I must avoid tangling it. I will try to live as
serially as possible for my child.

(No, that's not entirely true. Several times I have
bounced forward and observed him from a distance. But
only from a distance.)

On occasion I still flee to the house in 1999. But I no
longer do so desperately. I go only for short vacations.
Very short. I know what awaits me there. But I also know
that I will live to see my son reach manhood, so I am not
as fearful as I once was. I know I have time; so death has
lost its immediacy.

And the party has changed too. The mood of it is no
longer so morbid. Not even grim. Just quiet. Waiting.
Yes, many of these men have come here to die. No—to
await death in the company of others like themselves.
They help each other. And that's good. (I don't need their
help, not yet, so right now I can be objective about it.
Maybe later, I won't.)

So I'm relaxed. At ease with myself. Happy. Because I
know who I am.

I'm Dan and Don and Diane and Donna.

And Uncle Jim too. And somewhere, Aunt Jane.

And little Danny. I diaper him; I powder his pink little fanny and wonder that my skin was ever that smooth. I clean up his messes. My messes. I've been doing that all my life. I'm my own mother and my own father. I'm the only person who exists in my world—but isn't it that way for all of us?

Me more than anyone.

How did this incredible circle get started?

(Or has it always existed? Could it have begun in the same way the timebelt began—in a world that I excised out of existence? In a place so far distant and so almost-possible that the traces of the might-have-been are buried completely in the already-is?)

Many years ago I pondered the reason for my own existence. (*Why* "me"? Why me as *"me"*? Why do I perceive *myself*—and why do I experience me as "me" and not someone else? Why was I born at all? It could have been *anyone!*) It almost drove me mad. I had to have a meaning. I was sure I had to. Variants of me did go mad seeking that meaning—but only those of me who could accept the gift of life without questioning it would survive to find the answer.

I wrote in these pages that if there were an infinite number of variations of myself, then what meaning could any one of us have? I wondered about that then. I know the answer now. I know *my* answer.

I am the baseline.

I am the Danny from which all other Dannys will spring.

I am a circle, complete unto itself. I have brought life into this world, and that life is me.

And from this circle will spring an infinite number of tangents. All the other Dannys who have ever been and ever will be.

Who the others are, what they are—that is for each of them to decide. But as for me, I know who I am. I am the center of it all.

I am the end.

I am the beginning.

*   *   *

So, before it is over, I will have done it all and been it all.

I will take the body back to the summer of 1975 and lay it gently in my bed, to be discovered in the morning by the maid. I will take his timebelt and put it in a box, wrap it up for my nephew and take it back a month to give it to my lawyer, Biggs-or-Briggs-or-whatever-his-name-is. I will leave Danny the legacy of . . . our life.

Later I will go back in time and visit him again. This time, though, I will handle the situation properly. It's not enough to just give him the timebelt after my death; I must visit him early in 1975 and explain to him how to use it wisely. Especially in the case of Diane.

I've already spoken to the nineteen-year-old Danny once, but I felt I mishandled it, so I went back and talked myself out of it. Later I will try again. Perhaps a little earlier. May of 1975. Or April. (I must be careful though. Each time I change my mind about how to tell Danny, I have to go back earlier and earlier. That way I excise the later tracks, the incorrect ones. But I must be careful not to go back too early—I must give him a chance to mature. I think of the old Dan who went chasing after the young Diane. I must be careful, careful.)

Perhaps I should just leave him this manuscript instead.

These pages will tell the story better than I can.
Maybe that would be the best way.

* * *

There is just one last thing . . .
What is it like to die?
There is no Don to come back and tell me.
And I'm scared.
It's the one thing I will have to face *alone*. Totally alone.
There will be absolutely no foreknowledge.
Nor will there be any *hind*knowledge. The terrible thing about death is that you don't know you've died.
—Or is that the terrible thing? Maybe that's the blessing.
It's the jump-shock that will kill me. I know that. I will tap my belt twice—and I will cease to exist.
Cease to exist.
Cease to exist.
The words echo in my head.
Cease to exist.
Until they have lost all meaning.
I try to imagine what it will be like.
No more *me*.
The end of Danny.
The end.
I am afraid of it more than anything else in my life.
Absence of—
—me.

* * *

Dear Danny,

Time travel is not immortality.

It will allow you to experience all the possible variations of your life. But it is not an unlimited ticket.

There will be an end.

My body has not experienced its years in sequence. But it has experienced years. And it has aged. And my mind has been carried headlong with it—this lump of flesh travels through time its own way, in a way that no man has the power to change.

I've had to learn to accept that, Danny, in order to find peace within my mind.

My mind?

Perhaps I'm not a mind at all. Perhaps I'm only a body pretending the vanity of being something *more*. Perhaps it's only the fact that language, which allows me to manipulate symbols, ideas, and concepts, also provides the awareness of *self* that precedes the inevitable analysis.

Hmm.

I have spent a lifetime analyzing my life. Living it. And rewriting it to suit me.

I once compared time travel to a subjective work of art. That was truer than I realized. I am the artist of time. I am the hero of my own life.

And I can choose the scenes I wish to play. Even the last one.

And that scares me too. Just a little.

I don't know when that body was coming from. It—he tapped the belt and came back to August 23. *Thinking* he was going to witness the arrival of himself. Thinking he was going to witness his death.

Instead—

I don't know *when* that body came from. I don't know when it's starting point is/was/will be.

I don't know when I'm going to die. But I do know it will be soon.

I admit it. I'm scared.

But perhaps it will be a gentle way to go.

I will never know what happened. I will never really know when. And I will die much as I lived—in the act of jumping across time. It will be a fitting way to go.

Danny, you cannot avoid mortality. But you can choose your way of meeting it. And that is the most that any man can hope for.

Live well, my son.

* * *

Maybe this will be the last page. I think I should add something to "Uncle Jim's" diary.

Uncle Jim has given his life back to himself—that is, to me. Now that I know the directions in which I will go—no, *can* go—the decisions are mine.

I need do none of the things that Uncle Jim has described. (In fact, some of them shock me beyond words.) Or I could do all of them—I may change as I grow older. The point is, I *know* what I am beginning if I put on this belt.

I feel a wonderful empathy for that beautiful old man. And a terrible sadness at his loss. I wish he were here now. I wish there were some way to thank him, to touch him.

But I'm pretty sure the mere expression of the thought may be enough. He knows. I know he knows.

I attended his funeral this morning. I can't believe he's dead.

He isn't, of course. Not to me. I know where to go looking for him.

D

146

The Man Who Folded Himself

Should I?
The decisions are mine.
A whole world waits for me.
The future beckons.
Where to begin?
I am going to put on the belt.

About the Author

DAVID GERROLD was born in Chicago and educated at the University of Southern California, where he received a B.A. in Theatre Arts. He has been an actor, a producer and a director, and has written a number of novels published in paper and short stories for science fiction magazines, as well as editing several science fiction anthologies. He has received the Hugo Nomination for "The Trouble with Tribbles," an episode of *Star Trek*. He currently resides in California.